CREATURES

Gerald de Vere

Winner of the Bronze Medal in the category of General Fiction
for the 2023 Living Now Book Awards.

Third Place Winner in the category of Intrigue Fiction
for the 2023 PenCraft Book Awards.

Copyright ©2020 – 2023 Space Cadets Studios

In collaboration with Mental Anarchy Press

Cover Art by Monica Kay

For more, visit spacecadetsstudios.com

ISBN: 979-8-218-11193-9

DEDICATION

To Ash & Daniel.
For Chapman, Crichton & Oxenford.

ACKNOWLEDGMENTS

The author would like to extend his gratitude and appreciation to his test readers {you know who you are}, to Chase Will & Mental Anarchy Press for fostering this piece, and to publisher Space Cadets Studios for feedback in developing the otherworldly elements herein.

CONTENTS

EPIGRAPH

"Whenever any animal's behavior puts it out of touch with the realities of its existence, it becomes extinct."

— Michael Crichton

"Vero Nihil Verius."
{Nothing truer than truth.}

— Edward de Vere, 17th Earl of Oxford

1. ESCAPE FROM NEW YORK

On the third day: that's when it all came unraveling: when all manner of beasts clashed in the hollow, chasing me to this story's inevitable end.

But it's best to start with day one... August 21st, 2020.

That morning marked an end to twenty-three weeks of pandemic quarantine and kicked off a retreat into Appalachia that should have been liberating for my wild soul. Instead, it bent my mind inward on itself, shattering to fractals what was once a whole being.

I was already cursed with poor mental health – had been for most of my life, in fact. To capture my mental state briefly, consider me a depressed suburbanite-turned-city-rat philosopher: a hopeless romantic trapped in an imbalanced body with a knack for high anxiety and lowly depression.

Yes, yes... *another* one.

I'd been in therapy to deal with those afflictions for over a year, after persistent psychosomatic pains in my torso drove me to seek medical attention. It became quite apparent within a month of working with my therapist that the condition was nothing new. In fact, we were certain I'd been dealing with it since my elementary school days.

Perhaps I should backup. My fiancé and I had been quarantined with our roommate in a two-bedroom apartment in northern Manhattan for nearly twenty weeks when we realized we were circling the drain. We were stagnating mentally, physically, and – because it matters to me – intellectually.

We'd been doing our part to protest a corrupt system, did well to keep in touch with our loved ones, and we had the mutual support of our beloved roommate – our future best man at a wedding originally set for October 2020. In May, we had canceled it all and rescheduled for the following year, anticipating that the pandemic would persist through the end of that calendar year. I hate being right all the time… there we were in late August, and all was still shut down with no end in sight.

Despite our systems of support, the walls of that picturesque two-bedroom apartment were closing in around us… me. They were closing in around me.

So, I did what I hadn't had the courage to do five years earlier when I left my ex-wife: I packed up as many of our valuables as could fit in a mid-sized SUV and fled old New Amsterdam. Thankfully, though, I was not alone, for my fiancé, too, desired a change of scenery. We went from the most iconic New York City Borough to the outskirts of a tiny town west of Winston-Salem, North Carolina.

I escaped from New York… just like Snake Plissken, I had quipped internally when my father-in-law-to-be drove us across the George Washington Bridge, sneaking us out before rush hour in the wee small hours of the morning.

As fate would have it, my future in-laws had retired to North Carolina, where they had a beautiful two-story house with an extra bed and bath, a lovely little pond just over the hill out back, and a yard that butted up against a golden-green patch of virgin forest. It was as lush and as teaming with life as

I could've asked for, and I was elated to continue 'quarantine' in that verdant little spot.

Childhood as an indoor kid and adulthood in New York City made my brain itch for fresh air, sunlight, and trees. The concrete jungle had turned me into a full-blown naturalist and so I coveted the sanctuary of nature. I missed the wooded hills of home and the mighty mountains of the west. My goal was to be away from humanity – away from the unnatural asphalt of a decimated land. I'd learned in my early twenties just how rewarding the solace of the wild world was, and I yearned to find it again.

Nature reached out to offer ministry almost as soon as our nine-hour drive south concluded. It came in the form of a most-impressive Chelydra serpentina, or common snapping turtle. We had only just unloaded our things from the perky blue Honda when I noticed a crowd of the local children slowly gathering by the woods at the foot of our driveway.

I felt instant indignation knowing that the parents of these kids neglected to teach them any respect for my father-in-law's property, and I was cranky after the long trek. So, I marched outside, squaring my shoulders to appear more imposing. I knew the beard helped – that's why I kept it. It came in such great handy, tapping into the 'Daddy Issues' our backwards nation suffered from.

The kids backed away as my mysterious dark features bade them to give me space. There before them was the largest reptile I'd ever encountered in the wild. Sure, I'd seen certain species in zoos, but this majestic beast was far greater. Its shell alone was easily over three feet long, two feet wide at its broadest point, and easily one foot thick at its apogee.

"Do *not* touch the animals you find in the woods," I said. "But do encourage them off the road any way you can." Four out of five of the kids fled, but the shortest, most precocious of them stayed behind. She regarded me with wise old eyes that seemed out of place in her six-year-old skull. Her bicycle

3

helmet accented her furrowed brow as she peered up at me, perhaps facing her own Goliath. But I had no intention of fighting her. My interest was in keeping the snapper safe.

"Is it a monster," the girl asked, pointing down at the bumpy lump before us.

As the words escaped her lips, the beast loped out into the middle of the street. It heaved itself into a patch of orange sun where I could marvel at its full body. The shell alone was a work of art, with its mossy green peaks and muddy yellow undertones.

"Oh, no. It's not a monster," I instructed reassuringly. "This is a snap—"

"Stay back! Don't touch that. It's a snap—"

"Snapping turtle, yes. Chelydra serpentina," I asserted to the new voice parenting me from behind. I turned to the newcomer. She was a bespectacled lady, roughly thirty-eight years old or so. She was dragging a wagon with two flannel blankets loaded inside.

"You a scientist or something," she challenged. Whether her tone was annoyed or intrigued, I still cannot say.

"No, but I am a conservationist," I tried with a charming grin. She squinted through thick glasses. They magnified her tiny eyes and their darting, nervous movements.

"What's going on over here," I heard a man chime in from further down the street. It was a thin, balding white guy in his fifties. He approached like a curious pigeon, cocking his head to disguise his nervousness. I would discover later that he was the acting president of the Homeowners' Association.

The snapper loped along the street, making good time as it casually strolled down the line of cookie-cutter mailboxes. I watched in amusement for a moment before smiling and explaining. "Oh, we just found this old dinosaur roaming out of the woods. I think he's looking for the pond."

The man's eyes fell on the snapper. He recoiled, pulling his limbs close to his body in a sudden, spastic dance.

"Stay away! Those things'll rip a limb off!"

He wasn't wrong – I had heard stories – read more than a few books on reptiles. However, I wasn't too concerned, particularly because the old brute-in-a-shell had lost most of his upper beak, which made it hard to tell what he was at first. From the way he still had about a third of his face intact, I presumed the old terrapin had lost a territorial battle.

Perhaps, though, he bore the scars of victory. The well-healed lump of scar tissue could have been the sacrifice offered to survive an attack from a raptor or even a human. The snapper was quite the specimen, and its majestically large body offered up so many stories to the keen observer. I was in awe – I wanted to help it off the road.

"What're you gonna' do?"

"I intend to get him to the pond," I told the neighborhood president as I cringed at the sight of his white socks and slip-on sandals.

The Homeowner's Association president jumped back and uttered a screech that rivaled Fay Wray's shrill cries on Skull Island. This response startled the little girl, who finally ran home.

"What?" I was annoyed and I sounded like an exasperated preschool teacher who'd just forgotten myself in front of an unruly student.

"You're gonna' touch it," he asked like a child.

"If I have to, yes. I'm not opposed to that."

He trembled, quivering as he took note of the moving mound near our feet.

"Why don't you settle down," I sighed at the newly revealed man-child. He frowned at me. "He's just as afraid of us… and he was here long before your damned neighborhood was."

"Suit yourself," he said in a huff, "I don't wanna' see all the blood when that *thing* chomps your arm off." And with that, the esteemed president of the Homeowners' Association retreated to the confines of his garage.

Anyway, my scolding him seemed to amuse the lady neighbor, who introduced herself as Susan before she plunged into strategy. "So, I've had to do this before. The turtles and frogs come out of the woods to find the pond, but they end up on the street and I don't like leaving them to get squished."

"Of course," I exclaimed. "I imagine they're drawn to the heat of the asphalt for basking."

"Sure," she croaked. "Anyway, we just have to get him to crawl onto a blanket. Then, we throw another blanket over top of him. When the lights go out, these guys freeze up."

She had clearly developed this method from trial and error, so I was more than happy to learn while I followed her lead. Susan was right on all accounts. And she cared for animals… perhaps I was already making a friend in a new place.

"Next, we each take a side and grab the corners of the blanket. We're gonna' lift…"

We did and the snapper hissed, "and just gently set him on the wagon." We did, and Susan nodded with satisfaction. "Now, we just cart him down by the water's edge and set him down."

We lifted the snapper in the wagon, then Susan tugged it down the street to the southern banks of the pond, which offered public access. Susan also took care not to let the reptile loose too close to a yard with dogs. She really was a pro at catch and release.

Once we found a spot, we lifted the snapper out of the wagon, made sure he was turned to face the water, and lowered him to the ground. He did not move until Susan pulled the top blanket away, as if to complete a magic trick. As soon as the blanket was gone, the massive Snapper blinked twice, extended its tired old head, and clambered right into the water. I had the distinct sense that I had glimpsed the ghost of the Jurassic period's most popular denizen, Stegosaurus. The jagged crags in the snapper's shell, the stout but efficient legwork, and the head extended out front on a swivel simply took my breath – and my imagination – away to ancient times.

"Did you notice its beak," I asked.

"Yeah," Susan nodded. "Pretty cool."

"It's nice to meet another nature lover," I said, trying to be polite. "I didn't expect that down here." That last bit slipped out. I had gotten too awkwardly casual.

"Huh," muttered Susan. "Yeah, okay." Her words were quiet. Wounded, even.

"Oh, no – I meant…" she was already pulling the wagon up the hill to the street. "Have a good one, I guess," she said meekly, ignoring my stuttering attempt to correct myself.

Wow… minus two neighbors on the social scoreboard and I hadn't been in town for more than two hours. I didn't want to stand out quite so much… or so quickly.

I trotted back to the in-laws, my mind replaying the snapper in great detail. That wonderous stegosaur, with its missing beak, its elegant scars, and that lopsided shimmy, was the perfect welcome back to wilderness. I felt a calling in my bones – knew all my old adventures would come spilling out of me.

Sure enough, they did during dinner, when my story about the snapper prompted a sharing of tales from the Rockies with my in-laws-to-be.

2. BACK TO THE WILD

I failed to introduce myself. You see, my stories are always fully detailed, but rarely ever come out in an order that makes sense.

My name is Gerald de Vere. I realize I should've started there. I suspect I omitted it because I have always been subtly embarrassed of my pomp and silly name.

However, that had changed only a few months prior. At one point in quarantine, John Cleese, the great comedian of Monty Python fame, had hosted live video meet-and-greets with fans, and I was lucky enough to procure five minutes of his time. During our exchange, he informed me that my name was quite silly; sillier, even, than his own. No one's judgment from then forward has mattered to me. So, say what you will, and snicker if you must, but do know that I value the opinions of John Cleese far above those of my middle school bullies. Honesty is the best policy, and after years of being taunted for it, I'm done feeling embarrassed about my bloody name. Finally!

I grew up in Pennsylvania woodlands that were slowly and painfully sold off for housing developments as I aged, forcing me to bear witness to the onward march of our planet's most industrious parasite: humankind. Where, exactly, is not consequential, as I realized through my travels that we were just north enough of Pittsburgh that no one gives a shit.

In fact, most people in New York, when told I was from Pittsburgh, responded, "Oh, yeah! Yeah, I love the cheesesteaks." That's Philadelphia, on the other side of the state, and the culture there reflects the Northeast Corridor far more than my own backwoods of Pennsyl-tucky[1]. We also do American Football better on our side of the state. Don't be mad at the facts, Philly fans. It took that organization fifty-one years to win a Super Bowl; the 'Burgh won *six* in less time…

I had an overprotective mother, so I did most of my exploring through books and movies.

'What a cliché,' leaps to the tongues of the critics. They can fuck off. It's the truth. And it heightened my intellect – made me value facts. Most humans don't do things to make themselves smarter. I hope I'm an exception to that rule, but I have only my own perspective to consider…

Thanks to adulthood, outdoor adventures were no stranger to me. I'd been camping with Eagle Scouts, hiked the mountain trails of Glacier National Park, and roughed it without a tent on the banks of the Missouri River. Those latter experiences were provided courtesy of my ex's family, a wild bunch of rancher folk from the hills of Wyoming. Until now, I always had someone better versed in survival techniques to accompany me. I had, however, picked up on many of those practices simply by observing, or in most cases, volunteering to help. Now at age thirty-two, I was eager to test my mettle alone.

It was that urge that sent me down memory lane at the dinner table on Friday, August 21st. After my snapper encounter, I knew I must explore the forest flanking my in-

---

[1] A regional colloquialism used by Pennsylvanians to express how strikingly similar Pittsburgh's southwest corner of the state is to the culture and terrain found in Kentucky.

laws' property. I also anticipated their fretting over such adventures, so I decided to regale them with tales of my time out west.

My textbook fascination with the natural world had served me well in those occasions, providing practical experiences to apply my knowledge. One time, I was even able to point out to those cowboys that their herd was wheeling into a defensive circle to fend off a predator. 'Twas the following tale I recounted for them from my suppressed memories of Wyoming:

It was well after sundown in the rolling prairie just outside of Ralston and, from the back porch, we heard the cows bellowing[2] in an abnormally alarming manner. The youngest sibling, Jay, was first to react. He was a spitting image of the American cowboy, displaced unfortunately into the decaying West rather than the wild one. In this way, he was indeed a fellow victim of man's constant machinations. On that note, we understood each other, he and I, for in my heart believed I was a displaced poet of the romanticism movement.

Jay jumped on the only four-wheeler with a working headlamp. "Take my pickup," he instructed me.

Gladly, I thought. I loved those four-wheelers, but I trusted myself better behind the wheel of a vehicle with an enclosed cab: something sturdy and familiar in the impenetrable night of big sky country.

It was also a relief to drive an automatic after a tense day shifting gears in a stubborn, chattering twenty-foot-long 1956 Chevy flatbed truck {or 'How I learned to drive a stick'}. I hopped in the pickup, cranked open the window to let the cool night air in, and flipped on the headlights.

Jay-man led the way, requesting that I try to focus my

---

[2] Pronounced 'beller-ing' in those parts, I presume because of the sound the cattle make, for it is an agitated grumbling that shatters into honking. It has the same jarring effect as the screech of tires and crash of symbols on the street outside one's home.

lights just ahead of him to help him navigate. The rolling plains sprawled out before us like an overstuffed comforter on an unmade bed. Essentially, he had just asked me to run follow spot, which I had done for more than a few theatrical productions. Careful to follow his instructions, I kept just to the right of his quad and doused the hills with an electric glow.

We roved up and down the rolling acreage, interrupting the grass's feverish production of dew drops as our wheels slipped along the turf. It was only a mile, but it took ages. This was due in large part to our need for a steady pace in the dark.

We weaved our vehicles patiently through the foothills, the herd still hollering like operatically trained banshees. On and on they went, honking louder and wailing angrier as our exhaust soured the fresh alpine air with its tang. Finally, the pickup crested a hill and Jay zipped around to my driver window.

"They're down in the coolie. Drive up over the top of this hill until your headlights tilt down there. I'm gonna' ride around to the south and try to muster 'em out." He pointed to the path around our knoll, a clear divot amidst the hills.

"You got it," I affirmed, and lurched the pickup into drive. I eased off the brake and gently tapped the gas, rocking forward as Jay rumbled down into the agitated cows. To my horror, I knew exactly what the cattle were doing as I took in the scene before me.

One of my personal curiosities has always been paleontology and prehistoric life, and as my headlights doused the angus cattle, textbook illustrations of ceratopsian dinosaurs circling up jumped to the forefront of my mind. This method of defense, the texts all noted, was theorized based on observations of wild cattle and bison. As in all the illustrations, the calves of the herd before me were isolated in the center of a circle made by the adults, who honked and chided at the starry night sky. All was still, perhaps frozen by the breath of the mountains, but it was abnormally dark, for there was only a slivered crescent of moonlight to see by.

Fresh with condensation, the turf glistened in the headlights of my pickup as I enjoyed another deep breath of mountain air. Again and again, the ignorant heifers ruptured an otherwise peaceful night. Near the front lines, a stressed sow urinated in frustration, honking at her prone calf, no doubt begging it not to venture further away from the group's protection.

We had had two mountain lion sightings in the last ten days. Surely, I thought, it was worth being alert, especially given their formation. Jay circled them twice and one of the particularly ornery sows lowered her head and stomped forward at him. He swung the quad back up the hill to me.

"Boy, they're pissed," he glanced back at them. "You see anything from up here?"

"No, nothing I can see. But I can tell you they're circled up in a defensive formation. See how they're all facing out and the adults are protecting the young in the center?"

Jay understood my meaning instantly and, as he looked out over the herd, he winked at me. "Probably our friend the kitty cat," he grinned, knowing I wanted to see one. "Good eyes. I didn't notice that when we came up on 'em." I had, after two other survival situations that summer, made it a point by now to say exactly what was on my mind.

"You think the lion's back?"

He nodded. "For a city boy, you make one hell of a ranch hand." Somehow, this was affirmation I never realized I wanted, yet relished all the same. It still made me bristle with pride when I retold the tale a decade later...

ભ   જ

After dinner, I determined that the stage had been properly set for me to hunker down at the edge of the Carolina forest. I proceeded to unpack to a point of settling in before I dug out my rattiest clothes and donned them. My attire was intentionally comprised of the oldest work clothes I had: a ripped-up pair of black jeans covered in a palette of paints and a navy Henley that was thin but somehow hotter than hell.

"I'm off to explore," I reported to the family as I passed through the living room downstairs. "Please leave the back door unlocked; I shall return within the hour." Bloated with the gasses of digestion, they mumbled their consent from the couches.

I wasted no time in passing over the wire fence between the yard and woodland, plunging my busy mind into the nirvana of a hollow devoid of humanity. The humidity was oppressive, but I enjoyed being out in the sun. I had, due to my rolling waves of depression, been letting my belly grow. Sweating in the heat felt like honest work.

It was good for my soul, and the puddles of perspiration pooling on my chest put a smile on my twisted face. These were character quirks I had discovered in Wyoming, albeit far too late to appreciate the hills of my own home in southwestern Pennsylvania. I had vowed, upon my escape from New York never to fail in appreciating nearby wilderness. I was ready to seek it out: to disconnect from people and celebrate my proximity to it.

And so, I did, discreetly enjoying my pipe almost as soon as I had wandered twenty paces from my newly adopted abode. Relief set in as a modest column of smoke issued forth under my nose, and I kept my eyes on the forest floor as I unwound from the stress of a long day's travel. My plans to relax were set in motion, and I pondered through a half dozen stories I'd been brainstorming of late.

Under the hatched dapples of light that sprinkled across the underbrush, a black and yellow box turtle hissed, shaking me from my thoughts. So lost in my musings was I that I had nearly trodden on the sweet creature. I stopped, reassuring it I was a friend, and apologized for startling her...

No, I did not check the gender of the turtle. I have a male Eastern Box Turtle who looks after my parents back home. If you flip a turtle over {which you should not do unless it is your pet}, the shape of its under-shell will tell you whether 'he' or 'she.' Males have a concave 'scoop' that forms in the belly, which makes it easier to mount a female without sliding off her backend during nature's nasty.

A female box turtle, however, maintains a hard, flat tummy. Generally, with reptiles, fish, and birds, all of which I prefer to Mammalia, the loudly colored specimens are male. They display colors to impress mates. And this box turtle, while stunning, was much duller in coloration than several male specimens I had encountered before, including my own Slash.

I did not touch my new and startled friend, for I was concerned that doing so might teach her that all humans were friendly. That was not a precedent I wanted to set, especially given the reckless devil-children from earlier. I knew from anecdotal evidence that they played at the edge of these woods each day.

Instead, I asked permission to snap a photo of her lovely yellow shell. She extended her head towards me, craning to get a better look at my behemoth stature towering over her. But she did seem to smile, offering consent, and so I produced my phone and captured an image of her.

As I continued my hike, I came across the forest's stream...that vein of life feeding the marvelous creatures around me... and heard the croak of a frog. I eased up to the edge of the ditch that formed the stream's banks, but I was not so stealthy as the three frogs that tried to evade my detection. They failed, of course, and I waited patiently for the mud around them to settle in the crystal-clear water. I apologized for stumbling so clumsily into their paradise.

It was a one-sided conversation, but they seemed to comprehend my mild intentions through my reassuring, albeit alien, verbalizations. Refreshed after this pleasant exchange, the final arteries of stress from my ten-hour highway trek finally melted away. The walk was, in a sense, a scouting mission. I intended to seek peace daily under the protection of the trees; to make friends with them that they may offer me protection during my stay.

With this at the forefront of my intentions, I was drawn to follow the stream, which grew wider, its banks leveling out as it twisted north, deeper into the thicket. I also hoped to see more frogs, and so followed the stream further until its ramparts rose again. There, I admired its three-foot-deep mud and moss walls for who knows how long.

Creeping along, I heard two more frogs plop spryly into the water, but I was unable to mark them. Ahead, the stream trickled with more intention, and I saw it fork, leaving a bar of land between two thin waterways. Croaking indicated I might find more amphibian friends in the ecosystem ahead.

Wonderful, I thought, and I picked up speed. As it happened, that was not a good idea. I walked directly into a spider web. I had not seen it, and backpedaled, wiping it from my now-sweaty clothing.

Spiders fascinated me, but the way a web clung to the skin was unnerving – as suffocating as wrapping oneself in silk before rinsing off the brine of an ocean swim. Given the variety of spiders and the warmer climes, there was also a higher risk of encountering venomous creatures. I imagined bringing one home on my clothes and my skin wriggled. I did good to wipe away the web in my beard and on my pants, then paused to tuck my pant-legs into my socks.

Apologizing to the spider for my blunder, I backed up, deterred from that route. At least the spider was observed dropping to the ground. That meant it wasn't on me somewhere. Its abdominal lateral was most startling, spackled with mahogany and black, and crowned with finely pointed spikes. I later confirmed it was likely a spined micrathena or Micrathena gracilis, for those inclined to scientific names.

Not listed as poisonous.

I carried on, but thenceforth I developed a habit of crouching while pawing ahead of my face with my left hand like a child playing monster. Were I to be spotted in this hunched and silly pose, the locals would surely think me mad. As an outsider, I was already convinced they did. They had not been discreet earlier about watching us unpack our personal treasures: the plunder of eight years in the country's grandest metropolis.

In the privacy of the woods, I suspected a stranger might be more inclined to treat me as prey than as neighbor. After all, I was quite accustomed to being called a 'Big Apple faggot[3]' in small American towns. I detest the need to use the slur, but it's a cold, hard fact that I lived in a spiteful, machismo 'land of the free.'

For one thing, I'd been called that since I was in third grade, so I knew on some basic level how hurtful it was, even if it wasn't true of me. More importantly, it hurt and offended a good many people I admired and respected, and I constantly cheered for its demise. Whenever I heard the word, I always tried to debunk such ignorance, but reasoning with mountain goats never got me very far.

Joyful, stubborn ignorance ran rampant in my time, trickling down from the mountains like tributaries of man's self-wrought folly. Alas, until the patriarchy's homophobic attitudes evolved beyond such oppressive ignorance, I feared my species would continue to circle the drain.

I was an ally. Or at least, I tried to be. For the LGBTQ+ community, as well as the peoples suppressed as 'minorities' in

---

[3] The derogatory use of this term derives from late-nineteenth and early twentieth century America. At the time, it referred to an old, unpleasant woman: a metaphor for something awkward that must be carried. The idea that its origins stem from medieval heretic burnings {a reference to 'the kindling'} is etymological urban legend and had to be omitted from an earlier draft of this novella.

my country. Throughout my life, there had been many an asshole who questioned my masculinity or shunned me from heteronormative circles. But for every one of them, I could count at least half a dozen friends from those other communities who made me feel welcome, accepted and perfectly normal in my weirdness. Long live the arts.

I cursed myself for wasting time. I should've been inside writing something... anything. There was in me a tendency to procrastinate because I still hadn't found 'my voice.' I knew it was an angry one: depressed and frustrated with the hypocrisy that coursed in my veins – in the machine of society. No one would ever admit it, of course. It was far easier to blame their problems on the next guy or project their insecurities through judgement. That made people look confident. Humans loved confidence. They flocked to it... climbed for it. It was in an ape's nature to climb, and humans would climb any social ladder in front of them, never yielding a rung.

My thoughts conjured a tempest, and I grew light-headed as I ticked off examples, my fingers frantically combing through my beard:

Gordon Ramsey hurls his plated insults.
Joe Exotic says he wants to kill that bitch, Carol Baskins.
The Kardashians need more updates than a MacBook.
The Orange Man grabs 'em by the pussy...
The masses cheer. They mimic.
Like hyenas to a lion, they duck their mangy heads.
Like lemmings on the move, they tumble after fame,
And deep down, they know it's wrong.
But it persists.
Our race is flawed,
Broken and abused...
Social predators feast on pain,
And on all others place the blame.
Fall upon me, tooth and claw,

For it's too late to read my maw,
Agape it is, and so's your purse,
Tremble at my horrid verse!

☙   ❧

The tendrils of paranoia crept in as my thoughts pondered the fate of our species and old scars ripped open across the desolate waste that was my mind.

I was short of breath, though I was sitting still. Another of my many tailspins. How long had I been wading through that cesspool of pain?

I did not let these ruminations deter me any longer, and carried on at least another mile into the woods, stopping only when the throttle and chug of a bulldozer cut through my self-inflicted depression.

I ducked behind a tree, contorting myself so as not to upset another spider web. Pulling my handkerchief-turned-bandana over my mouth, I waited and watched. Two guys, anywhere between twenty-five and forty-six, trolled right through a distinct path in the trees ahead of me. As with many of the people I had come across previously in those parts, age was difficult to determine because girth or extra wear factored into nearly everyone. I felt all the more like a bandit from the old west, hiding behind my mask and noting that neither construction worker used a face covering. They both wore hardhats, making them an ironic pair in the churning world of the pandemic. Had Darwin ever conjured such a visual metaphor, he'd have been the butt of even more jokes than was already his fate.

Sunlight showered its golden beams on their pale, doughy faces and accentuated the ragged yellow hull of their dozer. Their coveralls and hard hats indicated that they were likely a crew assigned to building the new housing plans, thus permanently destroying the very tranquility I presently sought.

They were strangers to me, but with that realization, I retched at them more than the smell of hot August trash in Manhattan. What parasites we were. That one image of oafs on a bulldozer, plowing through my silence and shaking the fist-sized gravel trail, denigrated the remnants of my patience.

I had had quite enough of the follies of man.

This was a metaphor for my pursuits of solace in an expanding population of worker drones.

How industrious!

How proud!

There was another human sentiment to match the memory of trash bags baking in the sun in Midtown.

Suppressing my resentment and general helplessness, I redirected attention to the nearby spider web. This critter was strikingly metallic cobalt with distinct dashes of lime green striping its midsection. I later identified it as a basilica specimen, or Mecynogea lemniscata. I muttered to myself, asking God, or perhaps it was the spirit of the woods, or perhaps still Mother Nature… {I tend to think they are all one in the same and man's diversions make us look quite silly to the next realm.} …guide my path so as to avoid wrecking more spider homes. They were, after all, self-built – taking time, effort, and precision – all qualities I strived to work into my own routines.

The sounds of the intruding bulldozer died, and I carried on the remaining few yards from my hiding spot, crossed the accursed gravel path, and found a perfect spot to plant my philosopher's flag. The runoff from the neighborhood pond had evolved pleasantly to the stream, and here it doubled in width before me. The banks seemed sandy almost, and they again had lost their steepness.

Back on the other side of the gravel path, there had only been a few toads, but here there was a chorus of frogs – unseen but for shifting shadows. They croaked and plopped into the water from their perches. Vines grew roots from their twisted tendrils at head-height all the way down to the water, like the course whiskers of an old tree's beard.

Tall and imposing, the timbers had stretched their rooty digits likewise into the clear, running water. A seven-foot-long blue rock with strikes of faded aquamarine elbowed the water's path. This, I noted, would be a prime spot to spy the reptiles and amphibians that so attracted my fascination.

Perching on the rock, I puffed my pipe in self-satisfaction, making note of my present location and my passage through the woods to get there. I also snapped a few photos in the glimmering evening sunlight as it played off the rippling water, refracted by thousands of plump green leaves.

You shall be visiting here religiously, I told myself.

So, there I sat quite content, listening to the current trickle around that hunk of ore. It was the little things. I noted half a dozen spiders, including another spined micrathena, as well as a multitude of delicate needle-nosed mosquitoes. They made nothing of my presence, save attempts to feast on me through my clothes. I ignored them as best I could, swatting only at the one who jabbed his proboscis into a tender scab on my knee.

That hurt, you bastard, I complained internally so as not to break the peace of this physical realm. As if in response, the dull pocking of rifle shot thumped through the air like an amateur drum solo. I hunched down, tucking my pipe away, covering my face again, and listened.

The retort sounded again.

Echoing to me from the southwest, I affirmed. Just then, the sun's rays cast their pre-twilight blessing on the green children of the forest around me, and I took but a moment to appreciate the warmth at the center of our universe. The glow shimmered across the rippling water, penetrated the cell walls of the foliage all around, and I held the image in my mind, allowing it to gain foothold in my memory so that I might carry it with me forever more.

This light was the gentle and reciprocal probing that had

fed my world since the dawn of life. In that moment, the sun shared with me that it silently benefited from the view as much as I, if not more.

'It brings me satisfaction,' said the sun to my mind's eye, 'to know how long I have fed these creatures. They and I are one. You are welcome to participate, as I have fed your skin so infrequently these past five years or so.'

It had actually been eight years.

I had been approaching twenty-five when I moved to New York City after six years at university trying to decide what to do with myself. Not much held my attention for long, particularly on a professional level. I was about to turn thirty-three in late November. I didn't want to be reminded.

"Eight," I said aloud, thinking it polite to speak to the sun after such a friendly acknowledgement. "But your approximation is impressive considering that your life can be counted in *billions* of years." The sun's light chuckled lightly through the leaves.

Then the blasted gunshots popped through our commune again, reminding me why I was sprawled out belly-up on a rock, feeding the mosquitoes. Mostly this thought came to me hitched to the itching sensation gathering along my thighs.

I adjusted, sitting upright again. With another puff of the pipe, I watched a clump of toxic green foam go racing past on the current.

Was it glowing? I couldn't say, for the hue seemed to alter under influence of the sun. It could just be a cluster of frog eggs, wet with jelly slime.

A twig snapped under my heel as I shifted.

As if in reply, a branch snapped upstream of my post.

Was it just a deer?

Or was it the source of the gunshots?

I was being melodramatic…

Or was I?

Whatever it was, it was very close.

21

Fuck. My heart hammered at my ribs. Adrenaline throttled my limbs. I started shaking. Damn it all to hell.

I settled and silenced myself.

My breathing wisped slowly through my nostrils so I could listen to the forest.

I checked the gravel trail at eye level. It was about three yards directly behind me as I crouched on the rock, perched like a gibbon.

No chortle from the bulldozing beast…

Then, an indistinct voice drifted to me on the breeze.

Baritone in range, it seemed unintelligible as a crisp breeze rustled the whole forest from overhead to underbrush.

I slowed my breath even more, but the wind rolled into a gust. The brambles and trees rattled, shivering in response, the boughs creaking in the canopy above like attic floorboards. It was then I realized that the cicadas and crickets had ceased, further unsettling me.

Other mountain lion experiences had taught me that such an observation should trigger fear. A quiet forest meant a predator in its midst. Off in the distance, a train whistle decried its insistent wail as it cut through the nearby town. Upon the freight engine's second retort – yes, I could tell the difference between a freight and passenger train whistle – a sound much closer to the ground penetrated me.

It was the familiar low-end bowel rattling of a heavy bass amp in close quarters. I had been on more than a few video shoots for Brooklyn rock concerts, so the feeling was all too familiar, specifically since it felt close: no more than ten feet from me. There came with it a high-end pulsating, which reminded me more of my phone vibrating a notification in my pocket, thereby shaking the dust off my ribcage.

Uncertain as I was about the voice I had heard muttering, there was no doubt in my mind that these vibrations had traversed my living tissue and clattered my bones a bit wherever they were jointed and fused. It also, I was not ashamed to admit, rattled my mettle. I had, in that moment plotted a web-free course away from the creek. Like a clumsy, frightened deer, I bolted.

Under the vines and through their whiskery roots I ran, then onward past a bramble of thorns. I stopped short of my second step out onto the gravel road. Reluctant to turn back, I cut left, exploring in the direction I had seen the bulldozer coming from and, I might add, away from the stream... and the unseen source of that disturbing pulsation.

Concrete manhole structures lined the gravel trail, cylindrical monoliths of sewage that stood – for whatever reason – four feet up out of the ground. I cursed mankind once more, negativity seeping back into my ruminations, allowing frustration and depression to supplant the solitude and peaceful musings that came to me in nature.

The peace had been shattered, and uneasiness took its place. I took a few steps forward on the gravel, which crunched and cracked unkindly with every subtle shift of my weight. It gave away my position in an instant, grabbing at my lapels and shouting to expose my retreat.

I froze in the exposure of that unnatural corridor for no longer than thirty seconds. Then, losing all self-control to my animal reflex, I leapt through a thicket. Cracking twigs as I fled the trail, I sprinted back toward the house, southwest of my position. Despite all these details, there was only one that propelled me forward: that familiar sting of eyes on the nape of my neck... eyes with harmful intent.

Something... or someone... was watching me.

3. THE NATIVES

Face-first, I plunged into the forest. My full beard swept up at least three cobwebs as I weaved through the pillaring trees. By contrast, I saw the fourth just as my nose came upon it.

The angry arachnid living there flexed its foremost two legs before me like a gym rat possessed by testosterone. I shuddered to a halt, and then managed somehow to roll to my left, as I'd seen wide receivers do in football drills to avoid defenders.

The resulting gallop made me note how silly I must've looked in that moment: plodding through the timber in a frenzied shimmy, wiping away the proteinaceous fibers of predatory spinnerets. As I judged myself for looking foolish, I felt the glares of the spiders all around me. Nevertheless, I criticized myself, promptly stopping.

Having judged myself at a disadvantageous time, I commanded such an abrupt brake that I rolled my ankle in a patch of soft sod. The toe of my shoe then caught under a fallen branch as I recoiled. The tissues pulled and crunched, though they failed to produce any obscene utterances.

Here, it is worth noting that I had agitated my right ankle

only the week before, on my skateboard for a trek to the Washington Heights post office. This was my sign to slow down, so I limped along a bit, noting how the feeling of those eyes on the back of my neck had dissipated – perhaps two or three cobweb-collisions ago if I was being honest with myself.

Ankle in tow, I hobbled steadily through the underbrush, enjoying the striking visual of some tubular toadstools the color of fresh orange traffic cones. Perhaps the nearby spiders were close to breaking ground on a new thoroughfare for low-flying mosquitoes, I mused as I marveled at the fungal vibrancy. Within minutes, I could barely see the white trim of our house through the shifting branches of the canopy.

On the back patio, I sat sweating and soaking up the waning sunlight. I pulled out my phone, seeking to identify those spiders while they were still fresh in my mind. The one who had threatened to bench-press my nose was a white microthena {Micrathena mitrata, for those enjoying my need for specificity}.

I checked my pipe in my pocket, which still seemed to be in one piece, and sat there sweating and enjoying the drone of the birds in the trees. I tried not to hear their songs as gibes of laughter, but my ears and paranoia over the adrenaline rush made a strong case that they were, in fact. I tried to collect my observations. I was certain there were at least two twangy voices at one point.

Or perhaps that was the buzzing of the bloodsuckers? That unsettled feeling of eyes on my back – had I ever experienced that and been wrong?

Sure, I reasoned, but alone in exceptionally eerie situations.

Paranoia also causes that, another more scathing part of my conscience chimed in. On I went, reading about the spiders I'd seen and only retaining a fragment of it, I'm sure.

The experience melted back into my memory, filed away under 'outdoor excursions,' and I carried about the evening helping to unpack and reorganize the room we'd be staying in. A bookshelf in the corner, by our lonely back window, would become my desk. I planned to sit facing the wall so as to have the window to my left. This provided a view of that hollow I intended to marvel at for the duration of my stay.

My purpose while down there was coming into focus: I would be a warden of these woods. The Woodland Wizard would go about each day collecting refuse from his healthy forest, retiring to his tall tower overlooking the tree line. He watched for goblins and dragons… and local naughty children, I thought, remembering some of the broken plastic toy pieces I'd seen in the forest near the edge of our dead-end street. Those six kids were from at least three households, and they seemed to be outside all day.

I thought they would be my biggest frustration down there… little did I know.

☘   ☙

Feeling somewhat settled, I hunkered down for the night. Or rather, I should say I fell asleep with a book in-hand… which startled me awake twice by grabbing at my nose as I slept. At least, that's what I accused the book of in my stubborn, sleepy haze.

In truth, I insisted on laying on my back to read in bed. With the book held above my face, it was harder to fall asleep whilst reading because I would drop the book on my face whenever I did fall asleep, thus waking me back up immediately. I had always done little things like that to maneuver around my undesirable habits. I didn't want to fall asleep while reading, I wanted to read.

Nine hours of car trip fatigue won the battle, though, and I set down *The Cave and the Light*, a hefty jaunt through the history of Greek Philosophy's influence on Western Civilization. My fiancé was still in the other room unpacking and organizing her work-from-home space. It was, after all, not even ten o'clock.

Not to be deterred by time – which was, after all, a human construct used to measure the unraveling of events as the universe expanded – I switched off the lamp and promptly fell asleep. Unfortunately for the story, I must inform that I rarely dream anymore. Or maybe I simply release them before fully waking, but in general my sleep state is an empty black void.

Perhaps my raucous snoring jams the 'dream frequency,' but I don't claim to be an expert on such things. Regardless, I was not left with some profound dream to share, let alone a premonition that foreshadowed things to come.

I was, however, afforded the clichéd 'jolt awake.'

 CB   ⁣

In the darkest hour of my slumber, I recalled that infernal pulsing sensation. It thrummed through my chest again and rattled me awake; I checked my pulse first. Not that I was able to do more than determine if it was normal or accelerated. Apart from the fluttering adrenaline and tapping anxiety in my torso, my pulse was normal enough.

That's how Day Two started. There was no going back to sleep with a mind racing like a runaway train-of-thought.

So, instead I was up before sunrise with a tall mug of coffee in-hand. Time check: five-fifty-two in the morning.

Enjoying the sheer novelty of the option, I sat on the front porch, which faced almost exactly northeast, and decided I would listen to the animals and appreciate my first sunrise in this peaceful place. Something shifted in the woods, which ran along the side of the yard to my left. As I spotted the haunches of a whitetail deer and heard more underbrush snapping under the weight of her hooves, I exhaled some of that anxious clenching in my chest.

How strange, I now marveled, that I so quickly forgot

about that distinct feeling which had sent me running through the woods in the first place. Watching for the deer's head to pop out from behind a tree, I focused on the sensation until I could stand it no more: I grabbed my pen and paper to attempt to record those thoughts that stirred the cauldron of my mind. Those notes have, obviously, come of use since:

> *I was fairly certain I still wanted to be a writer... Don't we all, I had since found out. No, I relinquished those pursuits once I discovered how damning all my rejection letters were. For three years of my first marriage and for two years after the divorce, I had vigorously applied my writing to play script and screenplay competitions alike. Prose, you see, has never been my first choice, though it was my first love.*
>
> *I particularly enjoyed the way a script reflected colloquial vernacular and captured a time, preserved in history better than any capsule might. But it was hard to hack it if you didn't have connections. On some level, I've always glorified the lifestyle of the starving artist: someone whose work far outlives their own petty human struggles on this planet. There's a tragic poetry between the lines when the reader must bear in mind how unsuccessful these artists were in their own lifetime. Were it that I should be so lucky.*
>
> *Anyway, the writing submissions stopped when the emotional weight of expectations and electronic rejections became too much. Emotionally, I could not be exposed like that while also collecting shattered fragments of my person, realizing how much self I had sacrificed for a failed marriage.*
>
> *As I wail about it, I should take a moment to briefly clarify the circumstances. I left her – my ex-wife – because I finally realized I was being emotionally manipulated and abused... though it did take her repeatedly weaponizing sexual infidelity before I threw in the towel. After a year of emotional torment, I concluded that I'd never be able to make her happy. In retrospect, I think an antidepressant would have done the trick, but I also*

acknowledge that that's the pot calling the kettle black.

My writing rambled on a bit until another snap out in the woods pulled me away from that torrent of thoughts on my notebook page. The cicadas didn't cease their comforting drone, so I assumed it was nothing. I peered through the thicket anyway, my eyes drawn by the novelty of seeing a critter. The wham of a tired old pickup hatch startled my attention back to the civilization off to my right – the very thing that had haunted me for as long as I could remember.

The neighbors two houses down on our side of the street were putting in a deck to ruin my view of the pond. Secretly, I wanted to douse the whole thing in kerosene and torch it. But I didn't want to risk further harm to the already intruded upon creatures of these woods.

Instead, I watched with remorse as a wiry, blond-haired man of maybe thirty-eight unpacked his tools from the truck. It was so hard to tell a person's age down there.

People could be much younger than me but have a house full of offspring. Also, the food and comforts produced physiques to match, and the hot weather encouraged vices like soaking livers in alcohol to slowly poison the body into an accepting stupor. Drinking culture thrived everywhere, though, even in the city. It corroded the foundation of that accursed first marriage, and I'd done my best to remove it from my own life since.

This fellow, for instance – the foreman – had skin as tan and leathery as a good old belt, mouse-like teeth that were bunched in front, and a belly that was potting. A hard-working, hard-drinking drone, to be sure.

Enter Butch and Jim, as I would later learn to call them. They dismounted in their own way from Butch's 2017 Ford F-350 Super Duty XL: a diesel-burning suburban meat tenderizer, if you ask me. Butch had the energy and composure… and body language of either a wild boar or a very lazy bear. I could not decide. Suffice it to say, he could only be described as very tall, very slow, and very, very fat.

Jim, on the other hand, was as lanky and wild as his hair: a coyote with a lion's mane. I immediately dubbed him 'toaster oven Bruce Dern.' True and honest imagery; my mind was first struck by Jim's resemblance to Bruce Dern circa his role in the 1988 film *The 'Burbs*. Simultaneously, the angry cardinal hue of his hide conjured images of the red-hot Nichrome filaments that warmed my toaster oven. He seemed to scout just a half pace ahead of Butch the bacon-bear.

Jim skulked up to the mousy foreman well ahead of Butch, who was slowly bumbling with a plastic travel mug.

"Everything good, guys," the foreman asked. He sounded concerned rather than scolding.

"Yeah, Chris, it's all good," Jim said as he slinked up next to his mousy foreman. "Butch's wife again. Try to keep it hush."

"Gotcha', gotcha'," Chris nodded, shaking it off.

"First load of lumber is already out back. Drawings are back there, too. Grab a donut and take a look before we start," Chris the foreman instructed.

"Thanks," Butch said meekly as he passed.

"Don't you worry about it, Butch," Chris said with a dumb but friendly smile.

As I set about defining a morning routine in my new living space, I took my coffee and puttered around the yard to the back, overlooking the neighborhood pond. That's when I got my first taste of the scheming lies of Jim and his dear Butch. Little did I know how much of them I'd be seeing.

See, Jim told the foreman that Butch's wife made them late, but I next overheard him report the following to Butch, out back while they had their donuts in privacy:

"Chris say anything 'bout us being late," Butch asked.

"Nah. I've been pretty honest with him about Maggie. Just don't say nothing to him, okay?"

"Why?"

A fair question, Butch.

Jim's performative skills were impressive. "He thinks he's the only one I told. Makes him more sympathetic. Plus, you like the extra shuteye, don't ya?"

"Yeah," Butch said with a big, dumb grin worthy of Bikini Bottom's Patrick Star. "So long as he doesn't start docking our pay. Barb'll notice if that happens."

Interesting, I noted. I assumed Barb was Butch's partner. However, I was fixated on Jim's social puppeteering. He seemed quite good at it. I may have learned more about them then, but Chris switched on his air compressor.

Unfortunately, I could only listen in intervals, when the pressure built up and the machine's motor settled. Jim and Butch were jawing about all sorts of bullshit: The Chicago Mirage of 2016, the rioting in Seattle – which was garnished with slurs of all make and model – and Russians on the dark side of the moon. It was so fascinating that, for a while at least, I only pretended to write whilst listening to their paranoid brains riff.

The crew also had in their company a teenage boy with a bad habit of staring at the neighbors like an ignorant steer. I figured steer-boy's dumb glare was merely a banal side effect of my being a stranger in a strange land – especially one with a dark enough complexion to stand out among paler folk. I turned attention back to my pen and page and wrote:

> *On one trip to Wyoming, I ended up at a community reunion where I was treated as what I can only describe as 'exotic.' It was just the eldest brother-in-law, a native of Rome named Amar, and me, but we were embellished and multiplied by estranged paternal relatives.*
>
> *"Who are all those strange, dark men with the family," one had inquired to the sisters. Amar's complexion was of finest tanned olive and his figure was built for speed, not*

strength. He had grown up in the Mediterranean sun and his complexion reflected it.

I, on the other hand, was a mutt of nondescript bloodlines and had had quite a bit of the prairie sun that year. I have no idea how my amalgamation of dominantly Irish, German, and Russian genes conjured skin that bronzed in sunlight the way wood darkens with a fine stain. Somehow, a pinch of Italian and Greek didn't seem to be the culprit. Instead, knowing the time of my ancestors' crossing, I suspected much of the Austria-German lineage also had Turkish influence, because they all emigrated out of the Ottoman Empire long before Archduke Ferdinand was assassinated. But that is all conjecture. The only honest answer I can give for my genetic phenomenon is a credit to my maternal grandfather.

I'm old enough to have an interest in my lineage. I always told myself I'd eventually have a DNA test but had always faltered due to the blurred laws surrounding proprietary genetics. Perhaps it would suffice to look at the results of both parents instead, I told myself. That way, I would have a comprehensive idea without sacrificing my own genetic identity. Until such time, though, I'm simply American.

I hated that, too. Despite having the label 'straight white male,' I had been 'othered' from such farcical standards enough to be hurting inside as I watched the abuse my country was inflicting on its own people.

What a year.

So much of the issue was sheltered privilege and fragility: an unwillingness to simply admit that, in many of those police exchanges, the person killed probably would not have been shot if they were white.

What did old whites lose by admitting that?

Pride... and the delusion that everything they have, they earned. Meanwhile, states of the U.S.A. have been vomiting nepotism since before they were states, handing down family privilege and clinging to it as a God-given right. White egos towered in my era, possessing enough money to surround themselves in a false reality of pleasure-loving ignoramuses while criticizing the have-nots for the world's problems.

Steer-boy's accusatory gaze continued, suggesting, "I don't think you belong here, stranger." Although it had just prompted a page of scribbles, it was still alienating, which is exactly what he wanted.

Was I hypersensitive?

Or paranoid?

That was a chemical side effect of my pipe, after all. Like so many other fools of my era, I sought assistance from a substance to help fix my anxiety, a symptom brought on by the day-to-day trauma of eight million people in my space and only eight trees to escape to. I needn't share which, nor by which means, prescription or otherwise. Make something up if necessary.

Now, I've grown distracted with expository details...

Fortunately, the steer boy was quickly sent to "go get more nails. Make yerself useful. I'm payin' you." Chris's words, not mine.

Due to his stares, though, it occurred to me to 'rough up' my outward appearance. I would need to blend in to be out among the likes of Butch and Jim. Fortunately, I had my heteroflage[4]: American Football.

As I recollected where I had unpacked my Pittsburgh hats, I caught glimpse of steam rising from a dispensable coffee cup held out to the foreman in offering. Coffee. My brain allowed the body's urges to be heard over deep thought. My muscles and mind {and olfactory} all yearned for a second porcelain mug brimming with bean juice.

That, logic interrupted, and the ball cap. I prepped my

---

[4] A word of the author's creation which expresses any stereotypically gendered activity, display, or interest that allows one to blend in with the existing patriarchal heteronormative society.

favorite mug in the one-cup drip machine and trudged upstairs. Instantly, I allowed myself to lament this simple means of fashioning coffee. Already I missed the routine of a hand grinder and French press, both left in the charge of our roommate in New York. They had been, after all, his investments.

My hats were tucked in a linen closet we had used for our seasonal clothes… and my odds and ends. These were mostly collectibles I intended to offload via eBay. I chose my newest Pittsburgh cap, which I had been partial to since purchasing it back in April. It was a subtle outline of the team logo, so you had to be paying attention to see that I was identifying as an outsider.

Not really, I corrected myself, as my own team seemed to have as many fans in this state as the local one. Either way, in my experience most plebeians thick enough to heckle were also thick enough to avoid heightened awareness of their surroundings, thus completely overlooking my hat. Regardless, it felt dangerous to identify as a peace-loving millennial so fondly labeled a 'lib-tard' by the brains presiding over blissful ignorance. Verbal beratement served to define pecking order, so our goal often was to tear each other down with words. I tried to bear in mind that the best revenge was to be unaffected by such nonsense.

Tucking my hair under my cap, I retrieved my coffee and the book I'd been imbibing and set up a chair for myself on the back patio. There, I enjoyed a second cup of coffee and relative peace, trying to focus on the historical influence of Greek philosophers while the honks and twangs of morning carpenters drifted to me from two houses down. I mention that as relative peace only because I would have traded it favorably for what came next.

As if hot off a 1985 Radio Shack shelf, the reigning entertainment champion of urbane status made its grand entrance. Ladies and gentlemen, the Boom Box! Chris set it out proudly and the radio was tuned, whirring and whining at the neighborhood like a cyberpunk rooster. Unfortunately, he tuned it to the twangiest of pop-country lamentations. Fortunately for me, the song was ending. Then, the country rock D.J. dropped in Cotton Eyed Joe[5] for his morning sandwich scramble. With an audible sigh of resignation, I made it to the first chorus before shrinking back into the quiet of the weather-sealed house.

It was too damn cold in there. I retreated further – upstairs to our back corner of the house. I had awoken drenched in sweat, so I assumed that it retained more heat than the rest of the house. I tried to sit and read in my curve-backed chair: an antique I was offered from a deceased relative's estate. I had fond memories of sitting in it and reading for hours as an adolescent. Now, I had even more fond memories with it from time in two different New York apartments.

My mind wandered and I could not retain the names of the Renaissance philosophers I was reading about. Self-loathing pressurized my skull.

Based on recent work with my psychiatrist and some extended reading of my own, I had come to realize in the last month that I had numerous signs of ADHD on top of the anxiety and depression. Or was I self-diagnosing again? My fiancé didn't think so... she had been making her own symptomatic observations to support my theory.

Wrestlessness[6]. It was how I described a growing physical restlessness when my thoughts were wrestling with the grim

---

[5] The Rednex were a Swedish house music group who, in the winter of 1995, reappropriated 'Cotton Eye Joe' from American folk. Given their obsession with American folk and bluegrass, it makes sense that they found the song. What they likely did not realize was that 'Joe' is particularly acknowledged as an 'authentic slavery time song' pre-dating the Civil War. What's more, previous versions of the song, recorded by white southerners such as Dorothy Scarborough in 1925, include lyrics that paint a cringeworthy caricature of a black man.

[6] No, not a typo.

reality of a human plague itching at Earth's epidermis. I was not going to read or write successfully in that frame of mind. I threw up my hands mentally, but physically I merely put my bookmark back in its place.

Fine, I resolved, another hike through the woods. Quickly, I adorned my same outfit from the previous evening, and then hesitated before grabbing my pipe.

I had been trying to quit... well, cut back, anyway.

On this occasion, I also remembered my Leatherman multi-tool — another relic from my tenure out in Mountain Time. Smugly, I recalled how complimentary my ex-father-in-law had always been about my handiness around their ranching operation. I bet The Chipmunk hadn't received such praise. The Chipmunk, as he is bound to never be mentioned again, was someone of no consequence who, I must assume, had very little self-esteem. They were, for the moment, anyway, partnered with my ex-wife.

What *was* of consequence, though, was what I heard as I slinked gently down the side yard and towards the tree line. Over the din of Rednex, I heard Jim holler out a question to Chris. As the song ended and Jim's voice trailed off, I was able to make out the end of his judgement. "...with these lib-tards moving in?"

My ears grew hot, and I desperately held fast the cork on my bottled anger. A crisp morning breeze rustled the whole forest from overhead to underbrush...

4. SHADOW GROVE

The emotional hell of corporate entertainment in New York City coupled with anxiety and depression had put me into therapy; I was still learning to forgive myself: to stand up for myself in confrontations. But still my body trembled with even the slightest shot of adrenaline.

That bastard. His tone was unmistakable. The only way his sentence could have gone in that tone was clear:

"What's with all these lib-tards moving in?"

Shit-faced–, toaster oven–, Bruce Dern wannabe!

I dove head-first into the bush, my thoughts running off with more ideas to jot down later:

> I was in the process of admitting that I had fallen prey to emotional manipulation for a seven-year-stint. I had painted myself the villain for meeting someone else after a year chasing someone determined to pluck every petal from her marriage, leaving only the thorns and one shriveled, pathetic little leaf.
>
> As I mentioned earlier, I was a hopeless romantic, and so found beauty in the tumultuous aspects of our relationship.
>
> Or perhaps that was masochism.

But it would have never been enough. Nothing I did ever was. Different love-languages had sparked the flame and undiagnosed depression on both sides acted as petrol.

So, I left. Not in abandon, but to stop the emotional bleeding. We had spoiled, the emotions growing acidic at some point. I finally saw the cycle of reconciliation, followed by depression, fueled by a lack of fulfillment, enticed by the value of self through lust for others. It was only going to repeat itself as I peered into future potentialities. The fire had still been burning in her eyes, even though they'd been wet with tears.

None of that poison was present in my current relationship.

指   指

At this point in my ruminations, I had wandered a quarter mile into the hollow, where I unwittingly moved on into the Shadow Grove.

I decided to call it that instantly upon seeing it because no sunlight seemed permitted to pass through the thicket of vines and thin-trunked trees that grew in that eight-by-eight-foot patch. Their tallest branches barely reached twelve feet tall.

This sub-canopy tangled with the vines hanging from twenty-foot trees encircling the smaller trees of Shadow Grove.

Immediately, I had to set about cleaning up trash.

Shadow Grove had clearly been a teenagers' escape some decade or so ago. It bore all the telltale signs: crushed Bud Light or Bud Light Lime-arita cans, half buried alongside two twenty-ounce Mountain Dew bottles, one of which had clearly been turned into a do-it-yourself MacGyver bong.

I cussed the curs who'd left their litter. Nowhere have I managed to escape the refuse – the signs that man was poisoning the natural world – and my skin crawled because of it. When I finished picking through the mud and moss, my bag was full.

I always hiked with at least a small trash bag, as offering even that small effort was my way of thanking the living world for the sanctuary it always provided me. At least, I thought positively, I managed to fit everything.

I resolved that I was not done yet with my time in the hollow and headed southwest towards the creek, hoping to spy the elusive frogs again. As I stepped through the spindly branches of Shadow Grove, the hairs on the back of my neck danced with fright, charged by that sixth sense: survival.

I felt eyes on the back of my head again.

Though I had read many a case of intuition unreliability and was well informed on confirmation bias, my instincts in nature had never proven wrong. Slowly, I turned back to the grove, alarmed but wanting to look assured.

There was nothing.

I shifted as a shadow danced in my periphery. Was it just the wind in the trees overhead? Slowly and deliberately, I edged my way south, watching that patch of woods where the shadow had moved. Nothing pursued me – no snapping or crunching of underbrush broke the easy silence of a morning outside.

My mind wandered off as I navigated my ragged green Vans directly around a patchwork of fungi. I stopped for a photo because of their markings – the artful brown and white swirls of a latte. The fungal texture even made these patterns look foamy. I slid by them, satisfied with two close-ups I'd snapped.

At this point, I had completely forgotten myself and I stumbled face-first into an elaborate spider web. Springing back, I peeled the web from my face. It wisped across my eyebrows and tangled around my unkempt beard. Huffing extra air out through my nostrils, I wiped the webbing down and away from my face.

The spider, now a dejected architect, plopped squarely on a fat blade of grass with very little effort. Another gym rat spider, I noted, but far more bulbous in his rear end. He flexed like a New York cockroach, and I could almost hear his Brooklyn tough-guy ranting, "Hey, I'm weavin' here!"

Not poisonous, I reminded myself, plucking clumps of dead insect pouches from my bandana. Surely, they had been the gym spider's morsels, saved neatly for later. I made a feeble attempt to set them down near the spider. Catching food was hard work, after all, and it was Mother Nature's only currency.

Thankfully, I had contained my hair within the bandana. Otherwise, I'd have needed a rinse-off immediately. Profusely, I babbled an apology, cursing my clumsiness before my heart sank... the fungi behind me!

Dreading what I knew for near certain, I turned and peered back at the latte toadstools. I had tread upon or otherwise mangled only two of the two-dozen there. At the time, I did not look at this fact favorably, and my frustration with the physical self reached a seething bubble just under the surface, where it often stewed self-loathing and depression to a boil.

Instead, I took a breath and then a puff of my pipe. The forest – and my brain – slowed down enough for my tension to escape.

You're in the woods, I thought. Enjoy it. That in and of itself was proof of the progress I'd made in the past two weeks. I'd only just finished reading *Families and How to Survive Them* by Robin Skynner and John Cleese. It had cleared my head on a number of things about my psyche. Being able to stumble around in nature was freeing. To do so in a thicket of healthy woods teaming with life was exhilarating. This sanctuary of trees showed far more signs of life than the little hollow in William Penn's woods that had served as my backyard and, by extension, my home for all my developmental years.

It was liberating.

Though, the webs were becoming a nuisance, I admitted as a breeze rustled more web in my mustache and, by extension, my nose hairs. I came to the fallen tree; its roots had taken a mound of soil with them in protest. The tree itself even had green leaves still, I noted, and much of the soil was packed in around the roots to allow it to keep growing on its side. A horizontal tree!

That, I noted with a respectful nod, was survival of the fittest. I puffed again and rounded the horizontal trunk, finding that its upper branches hung over the very creek I sought. As I plodded quietly within two feet of the banks, three frogs flung themselves from their muddy lookouts, plunking deftly into the water. I strained to see them, but the rippling current and the sediment they'd kicked up in their landing prevented me doing so. Their figures had been distinct for but a second against the pervading brambles of the forest. A clever tactic for avoiding predators, I commended as I watched the sand swirling in the water. Good to see you near, my little fairy god toads.

The heat that day was already making me sick… though my mind also drifted as I pondered any meaning to the cosmos. That sense of insignificance… of being an accident – a fluke of the ever-expanding Milky Way – drilled at my faithless, doubting soul.

The sunlight revealed in the branches before me another basilica spider. Its brilliant green stripes cut through a glimmering metallic blue exoskeleton. I paused as I noticed how furiously the spider was moving… it had a pin-sized hardback bug caught in its web. It untangled the poor, wriggling creature from the sticky net that had trapped it and spun it round thrice as quickly as a worker in a production line, then dropped it back onto the web.

Like an acrobat set free for his opener, the spider deftly swung away from the hardback, arching over to the opposite side of its web. There, a mosquito had just collided head on with its own demise. Wasting not a second, the basilica pounced, landing on top of the bloodsucker.

Excited to witness the weaving, I leaned in. I was sure this bug would be cocooned and dangled, as the spider had just demonstrated with the hardback. But as the spider looked back up from its prey, I realized I had been witnessing an immediate meal.

The mosquito was gone.

Good riddance, I thought, itching a welt on my shoulder. Sunlight sparkled on the web as the wind stirred the treetops overhead. The hardback was clearly a less enticing meal, as it still dangled from its webbed noose. Or perhaps they don't spoil as fast, whereas I imagined mosquitos, much like soup dumplings on a rainy day in China Town, had to be eaten fresh. Though spiders are said to favor a feast on a bloodsucker, I had never seen the preference in such violent action.

Beauty was in those woods – especially in these wild moments – but also Death. I knew he'd find me there eventually. He always did.

I puffed on my pipe, my thoughts tail-spinning to the grotto where it pondered existence – a most dangerous place to be.

Meaninglessness crept in first… my own indecision regarding a plan for my future festered instead into nihilistic bullshit. At least I liked to tell myself it was bullshit in the hope that that made it true. Depression mixed with a firm grasp on history seemed to put me at higher risk of such runaway trains of thought. I carried on, trying to live in the present – bringing my focus back to nature. How amazing that I had been able to witness that spider in action, as most would have experienced it only in a Nat-Geo documentary.

Many people I'd come across thought those shots in nature docs were just lucky. No, the digital age had made capturing such astonishing moments much easier. It's not luck, its skill and patience… and hours or even *days* of footage. It frightened me how many people still believed media was a truth-sayer, particularly in our self-aware digital age. But we are all subjective little cogs in society's engine.

I sighed, brushing away a branch in hopes that aggravating thought would move aside with it. The more psychiatry I was exposed to, the more unpleasant I realized I must seem to others. Another heavy thought... from there, I set about edging around ideas to try and find a pleasant one.

Just then, I noted a strange clump of foam that drifted down on the water's surface, tumbling past me. Foam on top of fresh waters usually meant either amphibian or fish reproduction, and the color was most-intriguing – iridescent and wavering between a hue of ripe limes and one of new tennis balls. It seemed to seep its tropical color into the water, but only in a limited and oily circumference around the concentrated lumps of froth.

That certainly struck me as foreign, and with another puff I determined to investigate upstream. I had taken only a step or two before three birds squawked in the bushes ahead and fluttered into the air. A glimpse of something indigo caught sunlight for but a moment. It was four or five yards ahead of me, obstructed by a thorny bramble.

I parted a bush rather than rushing forward further and swear upon my life that I spied a bumpy, rigid blue crab claw. That couldn't be right; it seemed bigger than my own hand, and it was gone so fast I suspected my eyes were just playing tricks.

I waited, hoping the thing would reemerge if I waited quietly for a time. Instead, the ground beneath me shuddered with a slow and steady thwump... thwump... thwump – a gentler variant of the pulsing that had rattled my bones like a subwoofer the day before. It rumbled up through my legs, traveling through my chest, and I had to encourage my physical body to breathe through the tightness it imposed on my lungs.

Whatever it was, it rumbled like a tremor, and it seemed to be coming from behind me: back near the upturned tree. Or was it ahead of me? Slowly, I was drawn back to that upturned tree. Its trunk had already given life to three distinct types of lichen, each a different woodland color. Even though it was still alive, there were patches of dead and rotting wood all along one side. Fascinating: it was both life and death all in one husk of sideways existence.

Quietly, I stepped around the root-mound, but by now the pulsing in my torso had ceased.

I stood still, scanning the trees for the source of that low-end hum. As I turned to look back the way I'd come, a twig snapped on the other side of the creek — four yards downstream, making it a full eight yards away from my first glimpse of the rough blue claw. Was I being surrounded? My body locked up. The forest's choir of birds and bugs froze, like an orchestra watching hesitantly for a renowned conductor to raise their baton.

Not good, I noted.

I still had not moved a muscle. My eyes quickly dissected every angle of the green vignette around me. Intently, I stared over the creek in the direction of the snapped twig. Nothing moved, save the hairs on the back of my neck.

Damn, I thought, I'm completely exposed.

5. CLOSE ENCOUNTERS

At first, I conjured images of some backwoods ragamuffin prowling through the brushwood with a hunting rifle, ready to rid his woods of my pestilent trespassing. Surely, I would have spotted such an intruder by now. I habitually sought out lonely natural places to think. When a human was near, I was hard-pressed to ignore it, let alone fail to notice. Humans were adept at disturbing the very nature they hailed from.

Something shifted behind a tree: again, on the other side of the estuary. At that point, my mind stumbled on a more visceral possibility. These woods had been far more expansive not five years ago, when my hosts had bought their plot of land. Deforestation of such a magnitude, especially in the foothills of Appalachia, could mean a displaced predator. Though rare to the area in the twenty-first century, I knew of big cats that once thrived in the east.

Perhaps a panther or an Eastern Cougar?

My mind conjured images of a big black cat slinking stealthily around me in a wide circle. The intense adrenaline in me was familiar, as a camping trip in the Snowy Mountains of western Wyoming had once before made me potential prey for a big cat. Instantly, the cowboy's lessons leapt to the forefront of my mental marathon: big predators will study you first, especially if they're a distance from you. They'll move slowly to avoid making noise, often creeping as the wind rustles through every plant fiber available.

Obstacles!

My memory hit on that valuable footnote. A big cat would not go up and over a fallen tree, as it risks exposing their position and they do not like that.

I had just such a tree right there. Injecting intention into every precise movement I made, I backpedaled with a patient and deliberate air. Six slow steps and the root-mound was there to protect my flank from afar. Another three paces and I adjusted to keep the tree between me and that damned noise.

My heart hammered in my earlobes as I suppressed panic.

This was a dangerous predicament.

I fought the urge to run, knowing how quickly I'd be pounced upon if I turned my back and tried to flee.

What a sure-fire death sentence that would be!

The trunk was now twenty feet away, so I turned to glimpse the terrain ahead. Another ten feet and I took off at a mad gallop. If a tree got in my way, I angled quickly, zigzagging through the woods, putting more obstacles between the creek and me. More than once something behind me snapped a branch. I risked a glance over my shoulder but saw only the stern trunks of proud old trees.

Before my eyes, the verdant sanctuary was transformed into a Darwinian prison: an expansive green coffin. I hurdled a bramble, my pant leg snagging on a thorny tendril as I went. There, ahead of me, was the wire fence and, just beyond it the safety of civilization.

Depending on my pursuer's experience, a human settlement might not deter it. The pitiful, mangled line of chicken wire fence that separated the forest from the neighbors certainly wouldn't. I stiff-armed a cobweb, feeling like a running back closing in on his end zone. Touchdown, I taunted myself as I stumbled over that metaphor, hurdled the chicken wire border… and stumbled up our sloped side yard onto the front porch.

My mind still raced as a haunting groan echoed between the houses, the sound waves attacking from all directions. My adrenaline rapped at my heart again, sending it aflutter. I scanned the tree line as the screech shattered the neighborhood air again.

Slowly, I turned, laughing internally as a rickety old postal truck sighed its brakes in agony, coughing its way to each mailbox. As I cringed at the sound, I realized it may be enough to deter my predator.

The boxy white truck groaned on, its chassis clacking and its bones trembling. Waiting to catch my breath in the now-oppressive heat, I cringed at the truck's racket. It felt foreboding…

I must be in the opening scene of a film scored by Ennio Morricone, I thought, where the suburbs supplanted the Wild West. A Spaghetti Suburb: the frontier of melancholy.

I was unsuccessful in making myself laugh.

Shaken and stirred… and in need of peace, I went inside to lie down. Granted, I first recorded much of my experience to that point, for I knew it had the mark of something strange. Promptly after taking my notes over bacon and eggs {at nearly one in the afternoon}, I fell asleep. I napped until four or so, but about halfway through, I awoke to a tightening in my midsection, just under the left ribs. Whether they were psychosomatic or not, I could never quite tell.

Either way, I'd been battling middleclass malaise for years in New York, but the comfort of quarantine had made me round in the belly. I resolved to annoy the neighbors with my brand of cardio: skateboarding.

The hills and turns in the neighborhood were just right and the streets were quiet. I changed back into my ripped black painter jeans and put in my contacts.

I didn't like being out with glasses on because I never wanted to be punched while wearing them, and there was clearly an aggressive stupidity steeped into the men down here.

My psychiatrist qualified these worst-case scenario ideas, such as being punched in the face in a social altercation, as 'catastrophic thinking,' but I blame the reality of catastrophic inbreeding. Ignorance is not bliss; it is a disease, and far more people suffer from it than is excusable.

With choice music filling my earbuds, I took to the pavement. It was going to take some effort to get my sea legs… board legs, I suppose. I felt wobbly as I coasted down the hill midway through our dead-end street. Locking in my core, I found a good cruising height, steered around some gnarly gravel and reached the stop sign at the end of the street with ease.

There was at least one cop living on our block, and I'd spotted two other homes with patrol cars in the driveways. With the nation's problems heavy on my heart, the last thing I wanted was to end up in an exchange with an officer. I'd had more than one bad experience with asshole cops in New York City, and I qualified as 'white' on paper. Such experiences made me even more empathetic to those in my country who didn't 'check one of the boxes.'

As my wheels rolled along the pavement, I enjoyed the vibrations sent up through my feet and the punk rock musings of Blink-182. It was not enough to stop my mind from revisiting a recent police interaction:

> *Once in morning rush hour, I had a cop threaten me, going as far as to lay a hand on his holster while on a crowded subway car. At 42nd Street, a major hub in the New York City subway system, I had to transfer from the yellow line to the blue. When my blue train pulled up to the platform, this pig, who was riding with three other uniformed arse-fficers, stepped*

out of the train to let people off.

Perfectly polite.

However, once everyone finished disembarking, he just stood there in front of me. I was directly behind him, with at least four other commuters waiting behind me.

Unwritten social law in New York requires that everyone line up along the side of the train and wait to board. Some passengers would have to step off to clear the way for people disembarking when the trains were crowded. One never tried to go around those people who had cleared the way, because those people were already on the train to begin with. The punishment for doing so was, at minimum, a thorough jeering or shoving from fellow passengers.

So, I waited.

The people behind me waited.

The people lined up at the other side of the double-doors boarded, filling up the car. The officer stood still; shoulders squared.

"Excuse me," I tried to sound polite.

"What the fuck do you want," was the lip service offered to me, the tax-paying citizen.

"Are you getting on?" Despite my best effort, I'm certain I sounded at least a little annoyed. "There's a line of people behind you."

"Go around, you asshole," the meat slab barked.

Nobody, dear reader, had ever simply 'gone around' other riders on the New York subway and lived to tell the tale.

As I followed his instructions, I gently asked, "how are we supposed to know that?"

"You wanna' make something of it, smart ass?" Now, he'd boarded directly behind me instead of letting the others pass. He stepped in across the doors from me and turned right as I went left, rejoining a group of three other in-uniform officers. With his challenge, he placed a hand on the holster of his gun, his finger waggling near the button snap that kept it

secure.

On a crowded train at eight in the morning, he threatened me with his gun for bruising his fragile ego by pointing out a flaw in his logic.

That type of human, I concluded for the umpteenth time in my life, should not be armed or permitted to enforce anything. To make the matter worse, his colleagues stood by, grinning like baboons as their friend swung his authority around like a pool noddle.

If nothing else, it proved to me that the offended officer must have had a significantly shriveled ego. Maybe his girlfriend had even said so the night before, which is why he was in a funk and taking it out on me.

I shook my head and squared my shoulders, unwilling to be intimidated. Instead, I acted determined and disgusted.

But I said nothing.

Fortunately, the old man seated next to my handhold caught my eye and shook his head disapprovingly in the cop's direction. I was grateful for his presence. When he disembarked with me two stops later, he sighed. He told me a story about his first trip to the city some twenty years ago. A cop had ticketed him wrongfully for J-walking after three other pedestrians, including the cop himself, had done so right in front of this wise old fellow. He reasoned to the officer that he didn't understand why the cop singled him out, seeing as the cop and two others had already J-walked. The cop's response, he told me, had been, "You think I'm being unfair?"

"Considering what I just observed, yes."

"So, you're resisting me?"

"No, I —"

"You want to make something of it? All I have to say is you came at me. Who do you think they'll believe?" The old man shook his head again, reassuring me that I had handled it well, but not to let it keep me worked up. My adrenaline didn't subside until two hours later.

ଓ   ଓ

Not wanting to stumble into an exchange like that down south, I decided to use my arms to signal turns while skating. I would also, I resolved then, stop at stop signs. Simply put, I'd be a perfect neighbor and responsible rider so these crunchy old farts-at-heart couldn't complain about my noise or recklessness to the Homeowners' Association.

I secretly hoped they would bitch anyway.

My wheels rumbled on the cracking asphalt, and I relished in disturbing the peace. I spotted a hill I wanted to try out and turned right. As I did, a big white Ford F-350 pickup came trolling down the street behind me. I hopped onto the sidewalk and walked my board up the hill as I saw him signal to turn left onto the main road, out of the housing plan.

No need to create obstacles for neighbors, I reasoned.

The truck slowed to a creeping pace as it passed me. I kept my eyes ahead and trudged uphill after the crawling truck as it moaned to a stop atop the hill. Despite the peaceful, traffic-free main road, the white pickup just sat at the stop sign.

It didn't signal.

The windows were tinted so dark I could not make out its crew, but I had a hunch this was the same chariot that delivered Butch and Jim to work that very morning. At the end of the sidewalk, I waited patiently for the truck to move on before taking to my board again.

It felt less than good waiting for that truck to move. It coughed exhaust from its tailpipe and still the engine idled. A lump twisted in my throat as I wondered what the hell they could be thinking.

They'd definitely slowed down when they saw me. Knowing consumer-country brand, I suspected every pickup down here was carrying at least one gun.

Catastrophic thinking?

Blast it all, could I not shut off my damaged psyche for even five seconds of peace?

Finally, after I realized I was holding my breath, the truck pulled through and made its left onto the highway. I'm not sure what I thought might happen, but I am certain I was being sized up, at least as 'the new folk.'

Like quills on a goose, the hairs on my arms shivered.

The gossip mill must churn near my new spot at the stream, I noted playfully to snap out of my fears.

I dropped my board, and I pushed off down the hill at full speed. Cresting the middle of the road, I picked up even more speed, which I used to swing round to my right, where I faced another uphill challenge. I rode at a cruise on that momentum no more than ten feet before the cracked and veined blacktop forced me to pump forward.

A good workout, I noted as the familiar stitch in my lungs tightened under my floating ribs. Soaking in my next breath, I mounted that hill and hit a healthy cruise for a quarter mile. The pavement was smoother here, and the subtle slope down to the next stop sign carried me pleasantly through the T-junction. I hung right, and then pumped as the road roughened again, sloping up and out of the neighborhood plan. Noting the community pool, I swung left to stay in the neighborhood. With the pool behind me, I suppressed my frustration that I would not be enjoying it that year due to Covid.

First-world problems, I taunted myself.

Perhaps, my thoughts prodded, a midnight swim would break monotonous nights down here. Not long after, I heard talk of the cameras down at the property, which had been installed after the pool chairs were vandalized one night two years ago. Humans can't share nice things.

Left, my arm signaled.

Had I continued straight, I'd have joined the main country lane. As I concluded the left, my breath caught in my throat.

The white pickup rumbled back into the neighborhood

plan from that country road, returning from whence I'd come.

It roared on down the street, roving as though it was looking for something.

I pushed on to put more distance between us.

The road dipped to the left and downhill, a beautiful, freshly paved stretch of Eden for my ride. I crouched down low to the board, allowing for less wind resistance and more speed as gravity tugged me down the gracefully sloping street into the newest part of the housing plan.

Cowabunga, I rejoiced internally, enjoying the breeze that danced over my sweaty torso. Leaning down even more into the bend of the road, I gathered speed before a seam in the pavement marked older blacktop ahead.

I hopped the seam, feeling free as I noted how smooth this stretch of pavement was, too. I had to steer to avoid a few notches clipped into the road, but otherwise this was the best spot I'd found yet for cutting loose on my board a little.

My extra speed allowed me to coast all the way down the hill, halfway down the street to the next intersection. Had I stayed on the smooth and sloping hill, I'd have been riding down a steep hill into a dead end that would've sent me crashing through my forest.

As I swung right, I had to twist my trucks around big hunks of gravel and patches of sandy soil on an otherwise fresh stretch of pavement. I was in the construction zone now.

The obstacles were enjoyable, but eventually a spike of gravel caught my wheel and sent me stumbling forward off my board.

An object in motion...

Determined to practice more than I had as an awkward teenager, I hopped back on. It was notably darker than when I set out but couldn't be later than six in the evening.

I checked; it was seven.

I had lost track of time somewhere around four-thirty.

Time flies when you're having fun.

I cruised down the sloping street amidst the three sixteen-foot-high mounds of Earth that had been pushed into a painful existence by careless construction workers. The spread of this new housing plan seemed to be just two lonely streets, both intersecting: one from the neighborhood behind me, and one from that same country highway off to my right. The two streets continued past their intersection, each ending in a cul-de-sac circle of pavement. The lots were quiet and empty; no houses had yet been built. It was peaceful, at least in the same way a graveyard is peaceful because there are no infernal humans milling about.

After all, I noted as I took in the landscape, this was all a bloody forest less than two years ago. My graveyard metaphor was painfully apt. Long grasses and weeds had sprouted some time ago in the turf so that now they spotted all the clumsy man-made hills like a balding man's last shock of hair.

The winds howled through that valley, bemoaning the loss of the mighty forest that once stood in this bald patch of scalp itching to produce its glorious creations.

I had the entire quadrant to myself, so after riding the hill down into the turnaround a few times, I took to trying old foot tricks. I had never gotten the hang of much of any of it, so I was more than just rusty. With my footing and balance feeling steadier than before, I attempted an ollie. My confidence was high.

First one failed.

Second one was nearly there, then my third, fourth and fifth attempts all failed.

One more, I told myself. You'll get it on this one.

I did just that.

The nose kicked up, my back leg traveled up to meet it, and my front leg went back down on the board. I even stuck the landing.

That felt good.

I tried again and failed before checking my phone. A text

from my fiancé informed that, "Dinner would be on the table soon." So, I nosed my board back up the hill. As I did, I noted a man prowling down from the country lane on a muddy white ATV.

His head was covered in wild white locks of curly hair. I rode right at him, unaware that he was staring me down as his four-wheeler rumbled down the hill at me. He wore a plain white t-shirt, blue swim trunks and cheap Old Navy sandals. His vehicle gurgled as my skateboard grumbled up towards him.

I charged, noting his close shave and wild black eyebrows as we approached each other in this strange jousting of energies. As we closed in on each other, I could see that the whole of his visage, once of the Caucasian persuasion, appeared leathery and sunburnt: a wholly unnatural reddish pink.

It was Jim.

The old man met my eyes with a wild stare, and I nodded politely as was custom around these parts. Left with no choice but social civility, he returned my gesture of good will before veering left, off into the neighborhood – back the way I had come.

There was something timid in him, I noted after I refused to break eye contact. But what I saw before that was posturing and hostile: a sense of ownership. As he puttered away, I noticed the shotgun scabbard strapped to his back.

Christ, I thought, had I seen that I might not have been so bold as to lock eyes with the crazy bastard. I suddenly saw the neighborhood the way he must: the paved streets melted away to dirt and the houses morphed into an Old Western main street façade. There is no telling whether the horse ranch I skated past was real or mirage.

Consumer-grade cowboy on his community watch, I scorned: the proudest breed of Private Property Defenders. I didn't doubt there were other Mark and Patricia McClosky sympathizers in my reach… probably with bigger guns, too.

Strange, though, that in the end, he seemed to submit. I pondered that as I enjoyed the empty, homeless street with its mounds of clay and sea of wild grass. I knew the grass was doomed and the mounds destined to become filler around the foundations of gestating homes, but I wished then and there I could freeze that sanctuary of freshly paved primordial suburbia amidst the trees.

I resolved to visit the spot as often as possible and noted once more how dark it was getting. Lightning bugs came out to greet me, marking the way home to remind me about dinner. Time to head out.

I hadn't realized how much of my return would be made uphill. At its pinnacle, the sky was already midnight blue, and I was only halfway up the sprawling hill that arched left into the primary housing plan. If not for my board's day-glow green grip tape, I'd have had no sense of where everything below my ankles was.

Breaking into the conical beam of a streetlight, I realized how much I was melding with the shadows. I therefore walked the board up the steepest point of that dark hill, listening as the white ATV gurgled along in the streets somewhere ahead. I steadied my pace to catch my breath. The ATV drew closer, its engine mocking me as it echoed between each and every house.

I dropped my board and shoved off again, resolving that I should be going as fast as possible. I wanted to be moving quick enough to zip past Mr. Dern's cheap doppelgänger if he crossed my path again. With sweat dousing me, plastering my tank top to my chest, I forced myself to keep riding. Sweat gathered in my tear ducts, the salt burned my eyes as I kicked off again and again, up another hill. Next, I hit the cracked and cumbersome pavement that had been absolutely punished by water, craggier than a dried-up riverbed in a seven-year drought.

Jim and his ATV didn't cross my path again, though at

one point I heard them grumbling somewhere behind me. There hadn't been a headlight between the two of them, so perhaps they were returning to their garage.

The onset of night brought a breeze, which sent welcome shivers over my overheated torso. My clothes were drenched with sweat, my pants clinging to my thighs as I turned safely onto Redstone Drive. The board hit smooth pavement and glided all the way to my last little hill, which I conquered with momentum alone. From there, I rolled to the end of the street, coming to a stop at the wall of trees that marked the Hollow. They seemed to be standing guard for me, and I felt safe as I kicked up my board at the end of the driveway.

Back at the entrance to our own cul-de-sac, Jim's ATV went rumbling past again. I froze, for the street was not long and he could've easily seen me standing there at the end of it. Thankfully, he didn't turn to look.

Buzz. Snap. Thunk.

Snap. Buzz. Thunk.

I steadied my approach to the front porch, looking around for the source of that abnormal, murmuring heartbeat. Then I chuckled as I saw its source: a crisp, lime-green and turquoise blue cicada, Neotibicen davisi.

It was at least two inches long, bright, and proud, and it was dive-bombing face-first into the overhead porch light, which had been left on to light my return.

Over and over the cicada charged, head-ramming like a Pachycephalosaurs. With such fervor, it harmed itself repeatedly, as though it was desperately forging its way through the stony gates of Eden.

At first, I smiled, taking its presence as a sign that my non-human neighbors far outnumbered us. But as I climbed the stairs for bed, some old entry from Greek mythology wormed its way through:

Cicadas were once humans who, in ancient times, allowed the first Muses to enchant them into singing and dancing for so long they stopped eating and sleeping and died without noticing. The Muses rewarded them with the gift of never needing food or sleep, and of singing from birth to death.

My brain, however, only sang these stories back until Day Two died with my head striking a well-deserved pillow.

6. DEATH AT THE DOORSTEP

The next morning, I was jolted awake by another nightmare that shook my torso, reminding me once more of the pulses in the Hollow.

Why did I keep forgetting those experiences?

I checked my clock: five-thirty. It was still dark.

Alarmed by my mental slipping, I picked up my pipe hesitantly. I may be overdoing it, I told myself. In only thirty-six hours, I'd experienced far too much paranoia. My reliance on the stuff to settle my mind won the battle, so I took the pipe and quietly slipped outside.

The sky was dark and clear, and I found myself sitting back in one of the wooden patio chairs to star gaze. Its surface was wet with dew that seeped into the seat of my pants, but I ignored it, reclining as far back as I could to appreciate the clarity of the stars at my new post. Just then I had the great fortune to spot a shooting star. Thank goodness I did, for at the same time I noted Orion standing watch overhead. I had, I realized, not seen the stars, or even remembered to look up at them in almost a full year. There was far too much light pollution in the city that never sleeps, and Pittsburgh was usually overcast during my visits… it was overcast more often than Seattle, according to an article my dad had shared a few years back. Perhaps that explained my love of a rainy day and my wish for snow throughout the winter months. Perhaps it also explains the depression, I prodded myself for the sake of a snicker that didn't come.

Accepting the dew that had transferred to my clothes, I settled into the chair with another puff of my pipe. Laying my head against the cold wood, I noted a solid white light glaring intently at me overhead. I stared back, waiting to see if it would flicker. I had learned in middle school how to tell the difference between the light from a star and the light from a planet.

My eighth-grade teacher had taught me. He had been so simple and loveable, but his demeanor tempted kids to act up. Watching my peers undermine him was like watching a teddy bear try to maintain a friendship with his increasingly pubescent owner. My classmates were heartless, and I hated them for how they treated him. What a miserable and confusing age, I thought as my heart ached still a little bit for that mentor, who was surely lost to the great abyss of Death by now.

As Trey Parker and Matt Stone have multiple times observed, "Kids are little assholes."

Unlike my classmates, I tried to learn from him. Looking back, I realized it was probably due in large part to his enthusiasm. He was sharing his wonder at science with us… or trying to, anyway. We did a section on astronomy in which he explained the inherent difference between stars and planets in our night sky.

"If you watch a star closely," he had said, "you will be able to distinguish its flickering light. This is because the light is traveling at such a great distance and getting distorted in Earth's atmosphere, and the light can't shine persistently. A planet, however, is much closer to Earth, merely reflecting the sun's light off its own surface. The surface itself is not generating the light, and the light has far less distance to travel, so the light is steady." From there we discussed the different colors of light that different planets would reflect based on their atmospheres. Mars, go figure, was red and Venus yellow. I didn't in that moment recall the others, but I was fairly confident I was looking at Venus on that fine late August morning.

I stared for a bit longer, trying to remember the few constellations I had managed to learn and locate. Developing that skill had been on my bucket list for a long time, and I still hadn't made good on it. Before I could venture down the path of self-criticism and disappointment, I veered to contemplate my adventures through the woods. After zoning out for an indiscernible amount of time, I found my eyes wandering along the dark patches of the tree line. The moon spilled its silver light on only the outermost row of forest sentinels, their bark holding the light like scuffed and battered knight's armor. The dew clung to everything, playing off the moonlight. The sky behind me, back towards the front of the house, was growing pale blue along the seams of the horizon.

A branch nearby snapped... not the cracks and pops I was used to from fragile twigs, but a heavy branch. I peered into the darkness. Immediately, I needed to remind myself that those same patches of foreboding darkness had welcomed me, even summoned me in daylight. The entire energy of the woods had shifted. I tried to conjure the image of a deer snapping a branch in the dark. Another heavy branch crunched, and I felt the hairs on the back of my neck spring into action.

I reminded myself of the paranoia I was chemically inducing and tucked my pipe away. Glued mentally to the wooden lawn chair, I scanned the trees once more, focusing my eyes on patches of moonlight that dared penetrate the secrets hidden out there. No more sounds save for leaves rustling in the gentle breeze.

My neck hair did not relax, nor did my eyes adjust any better than they already were. Scanning the darkness anyway, I searched for the slightest hint of a recognizable shape I might use to excuse my fears, or even explain them away.

There seemed to be a vague geometric form, like a dark and open doorway, perfectly rectangular and centered in the trunk of a tree recessed deep beyond the tree line. I squinted, blinking to clear the anomaly, sure it had been conjured by my mind, but there it stood, maybe thirty paces from my present spot on the back patio. Shaking my head, I turned back to the stars and the moon, needing something familiar and light. It was only then, gathering my senses, that I smelled the sour odor of death. It was not the sweet stench of a carcass on land, but rather the curdled clear coat of dead fish poisoning fresh water. Something had gone afoul down in the pond, but I dared not investigate... not in the dark.

With a sigh, I resigned myself to the confines of the house, abandoning my hopes of meditative star gazing. I slipped inside, trying to avoid the shrill squeal of the back door's hinges. As I did, the microwave clock shined insistently in the shadows of the house, demanding that I know by its green glowing digits that it was only six-oh-one. The sun was preparing to diminish that quiet morning darkness outside, and so, without something to occupy my mind, I quietly set about making coffee.

With nimble fingers and precision movement, I procured the instruments required for coffee, all the while pondering the doorway in the dark, convincing myself it was my mind making up the stuff of Narnia. Perhaps the pipe and my taste in fantasy were stirring into a dangerous cocktail of the mind, I reasoned silently.

As the percolator sputtered the first drops of coffee into my cup, I retreated upstairs to tuck my pipe away and get my fiancé's mug from her nightstand. My coffee done, I swapped out the mugs and rinsed the reusable filter, prepping it with new grounds for my good lady's cup, which would not be filled for at least another hour or two, when she woke up. Then, my own hot mug in hand, I slipped out onto the patio once more. The golden light of morning was paling in a gathering fog, but still there was enough light to interrupt the shadows of the night. I stared off into the trees again, wanting to dismiss my strange visions with the proof of daylight. Admittedly, I also wanted to find the source of the decay, as I feared it might disrupt my senses further throughout the day. I was unwilling to surrender my fresh air, particularly after breathing city smog for eight years.

Taking my time to sip the hot coffee for a moment, I eventually ducked back inside, cleaned up the coffee maker, hustled briskly up the stairs with my fiancé's fresh mug, set it back on her nightstand, grabbed a pair of sneakers, and made my way back out onto the patio. Because I was in no real hurry, I carried my coffee with me, sipping it as I marched down the hillside through knee-high undergrowth, careful to avoid the jagger[7] bushes near the water.

A breeze kicked up, and the smell of rotting fish overwhelmed me even before I saw the carnage. Through the fog, I spied two fish, both as long as my arm, floating lethargically on their sides. A crooning squawk overhead drew my attention, and I spotted a turkey vulture leering at me in the branches of a dead but mighty tree. In my peripheral, another winged shadow craned its neck.

My God, I thought, ignoring the stench of fish, there were seven of those ragged scavengers congregated in the canopy. The smell of decay was extraordinarily strong, undoubtedly

---

[7] The more pedantic reader, such as myself, may try here to call out the author for more pretentious poetical and made-up language, but this is not a word for which I can take credit. It is instead owed to some nameless Yinzers from generations past who, I can only imagine, stumbled into a thorny bramble. Admittedly, I do not know which Pittsburgh phrase came first: the jagger bush or the jagoff. I imagine it was the former and that the latter a colorful insult born from the former.

tantalizing the big birds like a pot roast did my own olfactory.

As I shifted around the large pine tree on the banks of the pond, enough fog cleared so that I could see exactly why these winged jackals had all gathered. It was not merely two juicy fish carcasses this wake of vultures had their eyes on, but a veritable mass grave fillet. I gaped in horror at the glazed white eyes of dozens and dozens of bloated, lifeless fish. At least six of them were three-footers, easily the full length of my arm and as thick as my thighs.

Tears gathered in my eyes as my brain registered that these majestic beasts must've been quite old to have grown so large. And clinging to their slime in the cloudy water were another smaller breed, though they too were sizable. The smaller fish were nearly as big as one of my feet, and definitely thicker. The bodies bunched up along the shore where I stood, stretching out into the fog in both directions: gaping mouths of agony expressed back to me the horror I felt seeing their sheen dry and cracked already from the hot sun of the previous evening.

I knew the foam in the water was a result of the decay. Fish had a clear coat of mucous that covered their scales from nose to tail; it was called a stress coat, and it helped protect them from trauma to their derma. It's what made them feel slippery to the touch, and I was all too familiar with it. Not only had I maintained a few aquariums of my own in my early twenties, but I had served as the aquatic specialist at a pet retailer during my college days.

I've seen many dead animals up close, including my first childhood dog, more than a few fish from the aforementioned aquariums, numerous beautiful specimens snuffed out by vehicles, and even a few cows that had to be torched to avoid spoiling in the hot summer sun out west.

But I had never known such concentrated waste as that which floated listlessly before me. Anger filled my heart as my mind raced. I recalled seeing two gruff young men installing a drainage pipe between the pond and its much smaller counterpart just yesterday, on my neighborhood ride. That was at the southern end of the pond, half a block away. I cussed, knowing what kind of adhesives were used to seal PVC piping. There was nothing else I could do but string a line of expletives, hurling insults at their stupidity. I sipped my coffee to keep the rotting smell of scales at bay in my nostrils.

We are a careless, ignorant species, and rage flashed white across my vision as I drew my conclusion, thinking of how potent those chemicals must have been, of how carelessly those two men had gone about their work, their sweaty ass cracks exposed to the world the same way their blunder was now exposed to me despite the morning's foggy blanket. What else but a pollutant could have caused such sudden and stark carnage?

Seeing such things reminded me instantly of my own country's role in giving zero fucks about our oceans, our ice caps, and the poor creatures who were too small to rise up and strangle us in our sleep, however much we deserved it.

My rage bubbled over, extending to the vultures, who cocked their heads quizzically at my strange visage. I shook that thought away. They were simply here to do what they did by nature's design. Our folly was merely their feast.

With dashed spirits, I trudged back up the hill, sending a text to my fiancé's father. It was the least I could do, and I knew from talking with him that the pond was curated by their homeowner's association. The fuckers were lucky he was the one to contact them, for I would have torn open several new assholes in my foul mood. There was no reason for such careless slaughter.

But, then again, I reminded myself, humans can't even treat each other right. That thought conjured the images of George Floyd begging for air while Derek Chauvin knelt on his neck. From there, I spiraled:

How many privileged fuckers had seen that image and still came to the defense of Chauvin? I sarcastically supposed that that counterfeit twenty-dollar bill had posed a threat to Chauvin's pride. He was a parasite, letching all he could from his Wonder Bread world. It was unfortunate that I had to claim to be the same race as that wretch.

I said a prayer for George and his family.

There are truly monsters among us, and they wear our same skin.

7. HAUNTED

I needed a hike to calm my angry spirit. I trudged back up the hill and made ready for adventure, adorning my exploration garb. Feeling the need to forget the hateful the frantic machinations of man, I packed my pipe and slipped it into my pocket. It felt cheap and privileged to puff away those cares, but, in that moment, what else was I to do? Due to my own mental state {and my addiction}, I had no other way to unravel the day-to-day clenching and fretting that plagued every minute of my existence. One can only dwell on anger for so long before going mad for lack of resolution.

The clock on the wall pointed skyward as I departed once more out the back door, bound for nature at noon. Regrettably, Death was not done haunting me on that particular day. The warm glow of the sun blanketed me with an appreciation for life outdoors. With its loving rays on my face, I felt expansive: truly alive.

Then, I lamented the poor fish once more in their mass grave, as if my own enjoyment were something to be ashamed of. The poor buggers, I thought as I exhaled through my nose to clear the funk of their rotting meat. That was a cruel fate, to be sure. Slinking into the woods next to the house, I resolved to head for the stream.

That poisoned pond provided runoff to the creek, and my amphibian friends kept court there. Hopefully, the current would keep things fresh for them, I acknowledged. But I wanted to check on them anyway. So, off I galloped, my hand extended before my face, my back hunched over like some old crone.

Once I was a good forty paces from the house and the foliage closed in around me, I paused to savor my smoke.

Numb went my brain and loose went my muscles. The effect was welcome after all my angry clenching. Even here, though, the stench of fish rot permeated my own cloud of comfort. Eagerly, I lit the pipe again, keeping it close under my nose to avoid Death's cologne. Then, I pressed on, not nearly as worried about the things I couldn't control.

CŽ   Ȝ

All seemed to be in order as I approached the stream. The water ran fresh and clear, bounding over the clay-like mud and smelling nothing like the decay I knew to be only one hundred feet southeast or so.

The frogs jumped from their perches at my approach and, as before, I was disheartened by their fear of me. It was for the better, though, as I was the rare passive observer of nature's beauty, not motivated by the urge to rape Mother Nature as was the perverse tendency of my species.

There was that anger creeping in again, and so I took another puff, holding the smoke in my lungs until my mind coursed once more with peaceful thoughts.

Observing the clouds of mud kicked up by the frogs' hasty departures, it occurred to me that I had not yet attempted to cross the stream and explore further west. Just a few paces north along the banks, I spotted a ledge of grassy Earth slightly lower and closer than the three-foot-wide gap along most of the stream. Not willing to risk the repercussions of a four-foot drop into water and vagarious ground, I chose that bump of green to leap to. I stumbled forward, barely avoiding a particularly intricate spider web, one which was woven between two trees with tendrils laced five feet down to the ground. Easily big enough to catch me if it were strong enough to hold. That one just might be, I bemusedly observed.

Strolling further west, I kept the stream within view to maintain my bearings, though I did put some distance between us. It wasn't far that I explored before I spied something bone white in the underbrush ahead of me. As I approached, I realized it was bone white because it was, in fact, bone.

It couldn't have been more than a foot long, and judging by the rounded end, it was clearly a limb of some design. I fought the urge to pick it up, uncertain what disease may sit upon it. Leaning in, I saw the worn grooves where muscles once met to form a joint, and my mind ticked away the possibilities.

Too short to be from a deer, though perhaps a fawn? Perhaps even... my mind froze as my eyes wandered just a bit further along the bosk, where a small pile of bones was strewn about the browning leaves. There was no flesh or muscle left, and no skull in the mix that I could discern. No real clues as to the poor creature who had suffered such a seemingly undignified end.

It was too small to be a fawn. Perhaps a cat or small dog: maybe even a fox? It was impossible to tell, and that one femur, or tibia, or fibula, was my only real clue. As if queued by a script I was not privy to, darkness rolled in over the sun, a sudden mass of grey clouds shifting into place.

Generally, I am a fan of a good rainstorm, and have been known to traipse outside just to expose myself to the sensation, even mocking those who shrink away from it. But those dark clouds closed in like a bad omen. Shadows shifted around me and my awareness, if measured, would have buried the needle. Anxiety went off the charts as I let Death cross my threshold once more.

Dust in the wind, my mind echoed a whisper of the lyrical wisdom of Kansas. Suddenly, I was staring at those bones through a long and narrow tunnel.

Would I know when Death was upon me?

Had this poor creature any warning?

Was it a peaceful death that lay before me?

I doubted this creature had gone out calmly.

There was a second, smaller collection of bones three feet away. Two more leg bones convinced me I was at the site of a predator's meal, for they were the same size as the skeletal jumble at my feet. The scene suggested agony.

My head spun, projecting me to some unknown vantage point where my future lie in a hospital bed, sterile and surrounded by old machines, eggshell in hue, as had been my grandfather's fate... had been the fate of every family elder who had fallen in my lifetime.

Trying to get a hold of myself, I peered up at the trees overhead. So comforting were they, like wise protectors who stood strong and watched as time passed them by. I should like to go out in the woods somewhere, I noted, wondering how I might best avoid the ugliness of a hospital bed.

I wanted to be in the fresh air, with a view of Mother Nature's green glory. How sick, that we reduced death to firm beds in baren rooms, our bodies integrated with machines like some mangled Borg villain.

No, a hospital bed would not be my end.

With another puff, I used that firm thought to propel my exploration and bid the bones a peaceful rest.

Death traveled with me after that encounter, sitting on my shoulder, and discoloring my every thought.

The memory of my grandfather's passing, for which I had borne witness in the room, plagued me as I pondered the experience in detail. He battled rheumatoid arthritis from his mid-thirties straight on through to the end of his life, and I knew there were days when the pain was too much for him. I tried to focus on that: on the positive. He would've wanted us to remember that his suffering was finally over.

When the arthritis took hold of him, he had to slowly give up his favorite active hobbies: bowling, hunting, and swimming {to name a few}. Upon losing him, my grandma shared with me that, prior to the crippling and gnarling of his every finger and toe, he had been, "such a beautiful swimmer."

She had said it with more adoration than I had ever heard expressed between the two of them, and it stuck with me.

Jerry had a small but powerful frame, much like me, all bone and muscle, and he'd worked in the steel mills around New Brighton until his late forties, when the arthritis finally made the pain too great, and he surrendered to a permanent disability leave.

Very rarely did he let on about the pain, but as a young adult, I realized that my grandfather's body slowly tormented him on a daily basis, morphing slowly into a prison of aches and pains. Some days it wasn't so bad, but other days it debilitated him completely, and he would have to opt out of family gatherings. His own form of quarantine, I reasoned, and one that lasted for decades instead of mere months. There was a slice of perspective for people complaining about Covid protocols, I mused.

The jab didn't lift my spirits.

My grandfather's passing had been a release from his physical prison. The day he left this world was strangely settling for me.

When his heart monitor flatlined, the sun broke through the clouds outside his tiny hospital window. While I understand how insignificant that may seem, it was a dreary grey week in late December, just a couple days before Christmas, and the sun had refused to show its face for a fortnight. But it burst through the clouds and into the window, bathing my grandfather in a heavenly glow... and *only* my grandfather. Somehow, the rest of the room was still grey with bleak shadows.

That moment lasted a mere ninety seconds, coinciding with the flatline of Jerry's heart. And, as if on que, the light faded as the clouds reclaimed the sky and the nurse came rushing into the room. With the departing sun, I distinctly heard my grandfather's gruff but playful voice, so clear it felt like he was standing over my shoulder.

"Don't look at that... that's not me."

The whole family was gathered around his dead and twisted body, allowing sobs to tremble from one person to the next as reality set in.

He was gone.

His last breath escaped with such a great sigh that his chest cavity sank deep. So deep, it threatened to dissolve into the bed. But my brain had already detached from that. I had the distinct sense that I was interacting with my grandfather's soul. That was still embossed in my memory stronger than any of the images I'd seen on Death's canvas....

It was the closest I have ever come to witnessing the ethereal plane. In fact, no tribute paid at his funeral even came close to providing the closure he himself had offered me in his final seconds here.

In moments of doubt, when Death was perched on my shoulder such as today, that memory reminded me to hold fast to my belief that there was something beyond this realm. I often used it to dispel doubts and paranoia.

There is something more, I told myself as I remembered the moment again: something 'after.' I tried to focus on that, but today it wasn't working.

I hiked deeper into the hollow, and still Death was at my shoulder. I rounded a particularly wide tree and my thoughts shuddered to a halt like a subway train that had struck a pedestrian. Before me lay a mound of inky black feathers and scattered atop them, bleached white avian bones.

Another animal corpse?

I have truly had my fill of Death for an entire month crammed into this one day, I thought with a heavy sigh. The morbid naturalist in me won the day, though, and I knelt to inspect this macabre scene.

The specimen had been a huge bird, easily the same size as my dear Pekingese pup. It had been, without a doubt, a turkey vulture. Like the previous critter, the bones were picked clean, but this was no tangled mass. It was basically laid out on the forest floor as though it were a puzzle that a child was working on.

All of it seemed to still be there.

I located the skull first, confirming that my classification was correct. As I noted the slender, pointed nose of the beak and the thoughtful empty eye sockets, I accepted that there was, perhaps, some beauty in death, of an animal being properly reclaimed by the forest. As I pulled out my smartphone to document the chilling image, my anxiety fluttered, catching in my chest before bubbling over, pushing more paranoia up into my brain.

There was no shaking Death from me today. I tried to hold my thoughts up, tried to keep them out of the muck of nothingness that awaited all living creatures, but I couldn't.

Procuring my pipe from my pocket, I took one hefty puff and stabilized again. Then, I forced myself to stay and take photos. I marveled at the absence of flesh and muscle, surprised by the fresh air that filled my nostrils. I expected the stale sweet stench of decay, but it was nowhere to be sniffed.

This bird had departed our world some time ago.

Had the bird's own wake of comrades picked it clean?

Perhaps that had been left to the myriad of insects and grubs thriving in the soil? Based on the way the feathery mound covered much of the skeleton, it must have been the bottom feeders, but the thought brought me back to the seven hunch-backed birds who'd greeted me out by the pond.

I had felt their eyes on me before I'd seen them, felt their hungry gaze as I stood between them and the poor bloated fish. Whereas my own reaction had been sadness and disgust, the vultures' gaze projected sickening delight.

Agents of Death, they were.

And today belonged to them.

With that, I snapped one more photo of the vulture skull and decided to resign to the house again. I drew the last bit of relaxation from my pipe before turning back, wishing all the while I was alone.

The Reaper's smoky shroud was ever at my back, trailing me all the while, haunting my peripheral. In past experiences I had turned to scold the shroud, but not today, for he seemed to be at full strength.

Instead, I tried to pretend he didn't bother me, but my scent surely betrayed me.

I hope I have by now established the ease with which I could navigate wilderness, especially woodlands. If not, I regret to say that it's too late for me to revisit the examples provided. But it's worth noting again, for shortly after I had turned my heel on the shadow of the reaper, I completely lost my bearings.

Gloomy went the sky above
Back and forth, the shadows shoved
Haunting my peripheral
Freezing still my troubled skull
Pound, my heart, inside my chest,
Save me from the wicked rest!
On foot, through dreams, he chases me,
Feeding on psychology,
He taunts, he beckons, through the night,
Savoring my mental blight.

When he's done, I do not know
Which way I came or where to go...

Less than two minutes before my thoughts had gone knocking on Death's door, the sun was swallowed in clouds. I had already learned that, in this neck of the woods, moss grew freely on whichever side of a rock or tree it pleased, be that north, south, east, or west.

I surveyed the ground for any proof that the moss here conformed to northward growth. Instead, I marveled at how thoroughly it was spread over all things. In this secluded pocket of the hollow, the rocks barely showed any of their stoic, stony skin. They were all clad up to their necks in lichen, as were the trees, which had seemingly sprung up out of the moss. It stretched, clinging to their trunks like tightly fitted turtleneck sweaters.

The shadow moved again as my anxiety grew like a tumor in the pit of my stomach. My current plight was a perfect example of why I wished so deeply to separate myself from the smoke. I relied on it for comfort, but the truth was that physiologically it was causing shifts, heightening vulnerabilities, and preying on my mind.

The reaper's shroud floated closer, coming to rest just beyond my left shoulder. I felt him there, but his form waivered, billowing back to the limits of my peripheral.

"You are not here for me," I asserted aloud, feeling that it was an accurate statement.

"But I am always with you," he spat back. He did not seethe, nor did he leer, for he knew his remark rang true enough in my heart to fertilize the fear growing there. I turned away and trudged slowly but determinedly in the opposite direction. There was no real reason for this decision, though in retrospect my instincts must have known that hope of escape lie not through him, but with as much distance between us as I could manage.

"The distance between us is merely the distance between you and your own funeral," Death said, ducking out of the shadows ahead of me. "Every day, I am closer, no matter how far."

I averted my eyes and let my thoughts run wild:

Funerals: what a tormenting concept.

I had been subject to funerals from a very young age, and they were a source of mental and emotional Novocain. What an awful custom we'd fabricated. In the face of death and loss and sadness, one was required by societal prerequisites to dress in tight collars and stiff jackets, standing around for hours and forcing thankful smiles on strangers. It was hard enough to experience the loss of a loved one, facing Death head-on, but to endure social niceties from emotionally unavailable family members while strangers paid respects...

'Paying respects,' was a fallacy all its own. What respect did we show a corpse by desecrating it with preservation fluid, caking it in makeup, and locking it in a metal trunk six feet under ground?

The dead care not for costume.

Let them truly rest in peace; allow their bodies to return to the Earth from whence they came.

A funeral was not for the deceased; it was for the living. It was a way for the living to spread their grief and force others to come out in droves to masticate over the loss, compartmentalizing sorrow during a planned ceremony. What's more, by confronting Death on a schedule, most humans avoided thinking about it altogether...

Ten paces more and I was in the Shadow Grove, where the sky grew even darker. For the moment, Death had left me. The shroud I detected was only the low secondary canopy that grew in the grove.

Something the size of a dinner plate cracked off an

overhead branch and landed in the underbrush not two feet in front of me. Had I taken my next step, I would have been under it.

Another taunting gesture from my hooded rival.

Fortunately, I shuddered to a halt, grimacing as I stooped cautiously for a closer look. It was a snapping turtle, or else, it had been until recently. More accurately, it was the shell and stringy remains of a snapping turtle, the leg bones still sewn together with sinewy leftover muscle. The shell was impressive – ridged and bony – solidly two feet long from front to back. Overhead, a hawk took flight, abandoning the bits of her meal she didn't like.

I had always been an avid fan of reptiles and amphibians, stemming from a childhood filled with ninja turtles and dinosaurs. Most children grew out of that phase, but not I. No. Instead, I clung to my paleontological fascinations straight on through adolescence and into adulthood. Something about how patiently they continued evolving for hundreds of millions of years. Perhaps that's why most human cultures regarded them as scaly devils. The serpents knew what it took to achieve longevity on Earth, and they refused to share their wisdom. Nor should they, say I! We are a hooping, hollering lot: a silly bunch of bananas who poke and prod our way through existence.

For a moment, I admired the craggy edges of the snapper's half shell, even though it was upside-down, hiding its most impressive intricacies in the mud. Then, I spied the ragged flesh of what had been the creature's neck and saw the mangled head. One eye socket gaped with gore; the other eyelid was clenched shut so tight that it was wrinkled in fear. The poor thing's face was frozen in shrinking horror, a ghost of this dear animal's last experience among the living. My chest shuddered as I realized its pain, and I closed my own eyes to retain my swelling sadness.

I cussed at Death for toying with me so – for using this

poor critter to mock me further. I knew that birds of prey would ascend with terrapins and drop them from great heights to crack them open like nuts. The raptor I had seen had no doubt used that method, as there was little left of the snapper's under shell, and what was there was chipped and cracked.

Balling up my fists, I marched onward, having re-established my location by stumbling upon Shadow Grove. I adjusted course only fifteen degrees to my right so as to point myself back towards the house. Fortunately, even when lost, I had managed to move towards the neighborhood.

I would have eventually wandered to the tree line.

To spite me in my success, Death's action charged a new thought; The snapper shell could have killed me in a freak accident. It missed by less than two feet.

Had its barbed and bumpy edges cracked me in the head, I might have been lost forever in these woods. Though that was something I romanticized, I hoped it wouldn't come for at least another fifty-plus years.

"So close," Death hissed in my subconscious, the words bubbling up like poison in a cauldron.

I imagined one of the bony snapper spines finding purchase somewhere in my skull. I cringed as I envisioned my face shattering somewhere in an alternate universe where timing was less fortunate.

Perhaps I am too pessimistic, I thought, rubbing my scalp in appreciation of its wholeness.

Although my spirits had been lifted by those strange thoughts on my luck, Death was not trying to provide me epiphany. That was never part of our game.

No, next Death sent more sadness in the frailest little form.

Arriving home, I traipsed up the sloping clover lawn and made my way 'round back as was increasingly my custom here. The clouds rolled away as I plodded onto the back patio, and the sun caught a golden corner of rock. It was decorative rock, and some of the river stones were flecked with shiny mineral flakes, some silver, some bronze, and some copper in hue.

The rock that caught the sun flashed a deep, rich gold and I stumbled, thinking I was about to rescue a beloved piece of jewelry from the ground. After all, my fiancé routinely lost earrings due to cheap earring backs.

But no, it was a rock.

Before I stood again, I spied the delicate pinkish-purple flesh of a baby lizard. I had heard of but not yet seen evidence of the lizard population in this region. Having had a chance to consult sources, I'm confident it was a hatchling Six-lined Racerunner, or Aspidoscelis sexlineatus.

The rocky outcropping, the time of year... they lay eggs in June or July and the clutches hatch in September, so all the details confirmed my observation. Here now was my first glimpse – a delicate two-and-a-half-inch hatchling struck down while life was still fresh.

Dreading that perhaps one of my family members was responsible for unknowingly ending the sweet thing's days, I knelt closer to examine the little Racerunner. Starting at the head, I could not avoid noting the eyelids, clenched shut and expressing the creature's sad defeat. I found what I was looking for as I got to the base of the neck, where I spied a fine line of stressed flesh, not quite a laceration, along the body where the front right limb met with the lizard's torso.

After much consideration, I am still convinced that mark was perhaps from an altercation with a five-inch-long Carolina Mantis, or Stagmomantis carolina. I'd seen two perched on the charcoal grill the previous evening. As of yet, it hadn't been worth mentioning the mantids.

Unsure what to do, I picked up the little corpse with as much delicacy as my fingers were capable of. Knowing that the dogs trotted there regularly, I was afraid the fragile body would be defaced if left splayed out on the rocks.

Respectfully, I examined the little reptile, appreciated her markings and the delicate design of her toes, then it occurred to me to bury the tiny corpse and spare it rotting in the sun.

With this objective in mind, I scaled back down the hill, found a bare spot of clay soil, and dug it out with a big, thin rock sitting just an arm's length away. Tears welled in my eyes as I struck at the Earth with my primitive tool, and I chose not to fight it.

My sadness channeled itself into a gentle sob as I dug. The dead animals haunted my mind. I realized the only living creatures I'd seen on my walk were the vultures by the pond. and the raptor that had dropped the snapper shell. Death's allies, all.

Gently, I set aside my rock-spade and my throat knotted up: I couldn't find the little lizard's body in the underbrush. It must have toppled with the soil I knocked loose.

Had I buried it absent-mindedly?

I struggled, my hands shaking with panic as I tried to find the little animal. My selfish need to feel for the creature had so distracted me that I'd carelessly lost the very body I wanted to pay respects to.

"How clumsy," Death seethed at me from the edge of the forest.

Just like that, my sadness morphed into criticism and self-loathing. In the pit of my stomach, a cyclone churned, fluttering there like rollercoaster nerves. I was teetering at the top of a steep mental spiral. I didn't want to take that ride – not here, in the sunlight in the backyard. I was going to have to go back inside and interact with my in-laws, after all, and I didn't know how to explain these emotions to them... or to anyone, for that matter.

Finally, I spotted the little body seated on an exposed rock. How had I forgotten I'd set it right there? Was my short-term memory failing me, or was I just distracted by my emotions?

My heart was stricken with pain as I saw it again, eyes

clenched shut. Poor little creature hadn't stood a chance in the unnatural world human comforts were designing.

Death watched silently as I wept on.

My tears were dying by the time I finished gently packing in the Earth around the little body. I meditated over the site, half praying for the critter's soul, half begging that God would balance out man's selfish romp across the planet. My throat thick with sadness – and mucous – I packed in one last touch of clay and retreated inside.

The evening sky was grey, heavy with nimbus clouds that waited until night before they finally loosed their battering rain. I sat inside to collect the day's experience on paper. The rambling was cathartic, and it helped me to calm down, putting my brain back in neutral.

8. TEQUILA MOONRISE

I let the rest of the day drag by, opting to stay inside even after the orange evening sun cracked through the midday clouds. By then, I had recorded a good deal of my thoughts and felt clearer: more capable. Maybe it was just coming to a better understanding of myself – something that had not felt like my strong suit recently.

I decided I needed a distraction, so I called my sister. We'd been trying to keep track of each other better, even pre-pandemic, but we came from cycles that allowed excuses to build up, so it wasn't always easy. She'd been having strange but enlightening conversations with one of our uncles, but the new and numbing information they brought were taking a toll on her. So, we shared the burden. This all is crucial to my mental unravelling, so rest-assured it may seem tedious now, but as such things layer on top of each other, the foundation eventually can't hold the weight and it buckles, cracking all the way through.

I have already established my maternal grandfather. I have mentioned his arthritis. I have not mentioned his service in the United States Armed Forces during the 'Golden Age' – in the nineteen fifties. While I was always aware of that, he became particularly sentimental and reflective about his time there when I was a teenager. I suspect it was because he'd sit outside and share stories with my father – his son in-law, who also served in the army. We three shared all kinds of stories over the lawn mower. One time, my pap asked my dad if he'd ever seen anyone die in service, even in an accident.

My father had not, and we were both caught off-guard when my grandfather, with leathery tan skin and ornery hooded brow, grew somber.

"I did," he said with a slow, regretful nod. Nervously, he gnawed at the end of his cigar. While he was in basic, a new recruit had accidentally pulled a grenade pin and one of pap's drill sergeants dropped on it, belly first, to preserve at least half a dozen newly fatigued soldiers nearby. It was particularly shocking because neither my Pap nor my dad saw active combat, as they were enlisted during peace time.

According to my sister's last two visits with our uncle, our grandfather's rheumatism may have been a result of his exposure to chemicals during experiments conducted on young men out in the desert. To try to make this very long story short, my uncle and mother had both met with their primary care physicians over the summer. Each of them tested negative for rheumatoid arthritis. Their doctors explained how some autoimmune diseases like rheumatism were not just hereditary; they could also be triggered by prolonged exposure to certain substances or chemicals.

Perhaps this was why it had not been passed on to any of his three children. My grandfather's mother had it, but not nearly as bad. Also, important to note that none of pap's four siblings suffered from it. While the doctors were considering things like environmental pollution, another possibility seemed to sprout up like a weed.

My uncle met a man around town somewhere south of Pittsburgh. As people in Pittsburgh often do, they got to talking and the man, being only four years younger than my pap, had also served in the army... in the nineteen fifties... in the Arizona desert. His timeline was congruent with my grandfather's. My uncle offered up that factoid, which propelled the conversation into personal realms. Somehow or other, my uncle got around to telling the man that my grandfather once wrote a poem for my grandmother while he was stationed out there. He shared the title: *The Lost Boys of the Desert.*

Upon hearing this seemingly innocent morsel, the old vet's boulder-like body trembled as he wept. He explained that a contingent of the young men stationed out there were experimented on without consent, unwittingly exposed to various drugs and chemicals. The vet was fortunate enough that he was not one of them, as the military had ceased such operations not long before he enlisted, but he had heard stories in his time out there. Those soldiers who were experimented on took to calling themselves 'The Lost Boys of the Desert.' He implored my uncle to be in touch, wanting to share more, and they exchanged contact information.

"Let's have lunch," he had apparently suggested. "I'll tell you everything." After the conversation, my uncle coupled this information together with the explanation his doctor provided about rheumatism. I was unable to argue the logic in his reasoning, as I was creeping towards that conclusion myself listening to my sister round out the tail end of the story.

What's more, I don't put such things past the United States government. The United States, particularly since the dawn of the twentieth century, had been the world's greatest snake oil salesman, compromising morals to gain power, driven solely by the selling of defunct wares.

My mind reeled, as I'm sure my uncle's had; I imagined large groups of fit young men loyal in their green fatigues and eager to please. They pledged allegiance to their country only to be unwittingly exposed to all sorts of foul and hazardous substances, my grandfather struggling among them. They were kept like lab rats, told they were noble, but they were petri dishes. My grandfather spent forty percent of his life crippled by arthritis. It kept him in pain, forcing him to miss out on family events as he aged. He never made it an excuse – never complained out loud about the stares he'd get in public, and never used a wheelchair because he didn't want people to feel sorry for him.

"After all," he would reason, "I can walk fine." The unspoken condition to that was, 'when the pain isn't debilitating.'

Usually, a conversation with my sister left me in a positive place, but my head was spinning as I processed all this, and my mood was sour at best.

As we concluded the call, I made my way downstairs because we were prepping a birthday fiesta dinner for my mother-in-law, who was turning fifty-nine later that week. The actual date was still a few days out, but with a busy week ahead, we had decided Sunday evening should be designated for the big meal. We'd prepped quite the spread for tacos, even invested in some margaritas, which was especially exciting because none of us were drinkers. My fiancé and I enjoyed the occasional glass of wine or a margarita with a meal, and I'd have a beer or a rum 'n' cola at social outings, but that was maybe once every two months, if not less.

After my downer of a day, I was anticipating a stiff drink in the sun to numb my mind, which was firing on all pistons, depression serving as fuel.

Thankfully, meal prep made the rest of the afternoon accelerate, providing an escape. Dinner was followed by drinks in the setting sun, and all was forgotten until my in-laws turned in for the night. I helped clean up the kitchen, happy to keep my mind in a tequila haze. My fiancé and I sat up for a bit longer, until she grew tired and retreated upstairs.

Left alone with my thoughts, I began recording an account

of the day, stubbornly determined to revisit my grandfather's memory. I had no other way to honor him, and I felt compelled to do something… anything in his name.

Coincidentally, I managed to double down. I wrote much of the day's story… including all the musings about him contained herein. And the more I wrote, the more I drank. The latter was something he fought when his family was young, so technically I honored his memory and his struggles with addiction. I had two… then three… then four tumblers full of margarita from a pouch.

Capri Sun for adults, I jeered to myself as I poured the fourth and final beverage.

My brain was fuzzy; it was well after midnight, and I could no longer focus on the lines across the notebook pages. They twisted and twirled, intersecting like interstate off-ramps in a foreign city. As I pushed the notebook away, I noted that my feet had gone numb, and my fingertips seemed not far behind them.

As I stood, determined to check in with my physical being, I noticed the full moon outside. It was throwing hatched lines on the hard wood floors as it shone brightly through the wall of windows at the house's posterior. I emptied my bladder and decided to meditate outside.

The stark silver moonlight was welcoming, and I thought I might find some inner peace by sharing a quiet moment with it. But instead of Zen, I found more fear. It was tangled impossibly with the cords of sadness that had knotted up throughout the day. I couldn't stop picturing my grandfather, couldn't stop thinking about all the time I'd lost with him while hunting adventure and success.

It made me sick, made my head spin as I paced back and forth in the coarse clay soil. It felt good, grounded me as I worked it between my naked toes. I knelt before the moon, tried praying, but only the shroud of Death responded.

"The day is mine," he hissed.

I was too stubbornly drunk to run away after the day he'd given me. I was tired of that faceless, joyless ether haunting me. It had followed me all day and still dogged me in the new day's infantile hours.

I had just wanted to enjoy the woods – to enjoy my time communing with nature. Instead, I had mourned Death's handiwork, and I found myself emotionally drained.

"Leave," I said firmly to his shroud.

"I cannot," he said blankly.

"Then leave *me,*" I said as I stood.

"I cannot," he repeated.

Exhaling through my teeth, I whirled around to face the shadows in the forest and marched back to the house for my shoes. Quietly, at least I think it was quietly, I opened the back door, nabbed my hiking sneakers, and slipped back outside.

Death's shroud was nowhere detected, and so I carried on. While I cannot fully remember, I am almost certain I put my shoes on before sadness overtook me, driving me to hug the first tree I came to at the edge of the yard… quite literally. Sadness welled up in my chest as my mind reviewed all the beautiful critters I'd found dead that day. The emotions mutated into that familiar guilt of being human – of understanding that I was a tool of destruction.

Recently, those critters had lost a natural home, not five years ago since the neighborhood was sold and erected. I was all too familiar with how unnatural my species made the world, and I hated it. We had poisoned the well of creation. We were losing touch with everything natural about existence. I wished for a miracle – a way to go back in time so I could run free without worrying about who 'owned' the land I was on.

What a sophomoric concept, I thought. The Earth owns us – we come from it, and in death it consumes us – reclaims us. We are forever at its mercy. Yet we torment it, cramming ourselves into boxes away from the sun and the trees.

My skin crawled, wishing for the verdant freedom of

Earth before humankind. Tears rolled freely down my cheeks as I gasped for that liberty while grasping tree bark. It was with that thought that I leapt into the woods in my murk of drunken depression.

9. FIRST CONTACT

At the fence, I slipped up and over along a run of wire that had some give at the top. It was easier to bend the fence down at that point, and so I did. Once over the fence, I surveyed the scene.

Silver moonlight trickled through the branches like spotlights from heaven's mezzanine, inking the forest in peaceful blue hues. But I knew that's how nature worked; the angry march of life wanted me to be content – wanted me to feel safe. I stood, staggering in a fermented haze as I turned a full one-hundred-and-eighty degrees.

Something was behind me. It was a distinct sense; there was not a question in my mind.

I took to my feet, moving intently but not hurriedly. It was nigh six paces before that insistent, calming pulse rolled through me. My core shuddered, and I nearly doubled over. As I felt the rumbling, every other instance of the sensation came back to me, dreams attacking like starving crows, flapping their wings in my face so their visions would haunt me.

Over and over, I'd experienced it, not sure it was an external force. It was definitely external, I affirmed as it passed through me again. But now I was close to the source. I could feel it emanating from behind a tree ten paces to my left.

Another pulse. The things I feared were trivial; I knew that truth as my skeleton chattered in its musculature. I reeled around to my left, planting my feet and facing the source of the soul-draining pulse.

I stared into the darkness. Then I saw it: the doorway. It was a perfect rectangle seemingly cut into the middle of a sturdy tree trunk. It was perfectly plain, staring back like the doorway to a secret room in a mysterious old house.

I took two steps closer.

The doorway was blank: empty inside. No… that was wrong – it was a membrane of some kind, but it seemed to adhere to the curve in the bark of the tree.

Another thumping wave went through me, hitting my chest first and traveling out from my sternum. It was safe here. I didn't need to run.

What the hell was happening to me? Every fiber of my being told me this was, indeed, not safe: that I should already be sprinting back to the house. I blinked, convinced that the doorway was a mirage, but the impression stayed with me no matter how I moved to shake it.

Perhaps my eyes were not fooling me.

The doorway was there.

The darkness I saw clearly trimmed the doorway into another room. It did not move, so I plowed ahead for closer inspection.

In retrospect, it's embarrassing to realize how irresponsible that trip into the woods was at night. Not only was I ill-prepared, but I was also improperly dressed to protect myself against the critters of the underbrush. The drinking had made me forget all about the spiderwebs and somehow, I didn't run into any. Otherwise, I may have remembered to double back before plunging headfirst into the wild woods in a tank top and a pair of linen shorts.

I took stock of how noisy my passage had been up to that point. Immediately, I slowed to a crawl, toeing the path for branches so I wouldn't snap them. After some progress, I looked up to check my distance traveled. Very suddenly I realized the importance of allowing the forest its nighttime stillness.

The doorway was still there, but it appeared much smaller now that I was near. What had looked like an empty, human-sized doorway from the edge of the woods seemed now to be only three feet tall and nearly the full width of the tree trunk it was a part of. I had also been wrong about it being an empty doorway, for through the perfect rectangular opening, I saw a vast starfield beyond a slimy dark green membrane that oozed yellow-green foam.

What the hell was in that margarita mix?

Like any good ape, my first instinct was to reach out toward the gelatinous membrane in the doorway. It shimmered in the full moonlight, which had morphed a sickly mint green under the forest's canopy.

'Don't,' a voice commanded in my head. It wasn't Death; it didn't hiss like Death.

Was it God? Did I still believe in such things?

'No,' the voice replied firmly.

That's about when I noticed the basketball-sized indigo crustacean perched on a nearby rock at the base of a great oak tree.

I blinked.

It was still there; one giant, bloodshot yellow eye throbbing in the center of its crab-like head.

My breath snagged in my panicked chest, where my heart was aflutter like a caged bat. Lightheaded, I struggled to keep my eyes focused. They wanted to go crossed, as though that might break the illusion before me.

'I am Grāf,' it said in my head. Instinctively, I grabbed and scratched at my ears. The damn thing was in my brain.

I never wanted bagged tequila again.

Had it gone bad?

Is that why the whole family went to sleep early?

Would I find them all dead later?

'It is unlikely,' the creature's little voice rang out through my mental thunder. I couldn't believe it.

"How do you speak English," was the first thought I blurted out.

Surely, I had caught a continuity error conjured in my mind. Grāf was merely mirage.

'I am not,' the creature insisted. 'I can communicate because I have been studying your thought patterns internally... I am Grāf.'

"Bullshit," I sputtered ignorantly, "you can't be real. I can't actually hear you." Adrenaline coursed through me, making ribbons of my muscles.

How I wished I had my pipe. Or was that part of this unraveling, too? With a deep and shaky breath, I forced myself to look the creature in its lonesome eye. The sickly yellow thing was massive, roughly the size of a softball, and its diamond-shaped pupil was unsettling. It protruded at the top front of the thing's hard blue shell.

I counted eight legs, perhaps a delusion from my time with the spiders, but each leg on this beast seemed much like a crab's. Unlike a crab's, however, every single leg had had a claw at the end, and the appendages opened a full one-hundred-and-eighty degrees so they could act as feet.

I watched as the thing shifted, raising one leg on each side of its body, and clamping the claws closed.

The indigo hue of its crusty carapace was as mesmerizing as the night sky under the Rockies, but its most distracting feature was nestled at its posterior, behind that big, ugly eye. In its rear, Grāf's exoskeleton had an open compartment that fanned out like a clam shell. There, where Earthly creatures fart and shit, this strange new beast stored its brain.

Green and shriveled, the little butt-brain was tethered in place by a tangle of pulsating veins. It all fit quite snug there in the scoop of the clam-like compartment, and I noted the toxic green mucous that leaked from its wrinkles as Grāf spoke again. 'I communicate through direct thought.' It waggled its brain-butt at me.

"No way," I shook my head. "You'd never survive on an evolutionary chain with such a sensitive area exposed like that."

Without 'saying' a word, the critter clapped its posterior clamshell shut, encasing its brain safely inside its prickly blue exoskeleton. It dropped back on four claws, raised the front four legs, and snapped the claws, then bared a vertical maw of needle teeth inside a spider's chelicera.

"That'll do it," I surrendered. I considered that the thing before me might truly be real. I was certainly in no condition to be making up mucous-soaked brain butts in crab shells. "So," I pieced together slowly, "the, uh, thumping that shook my insides... that was you?"

I was thankful that my voice didn't betray my quivering insides. My brain felt as though it might unfurl inside out as I choked the coherent thought forward.

The thing called Grāf lowered its threatening claws, spreading them back into feet. It shuffled its chelicera, clicking those needle-teeth off one another. Next, the clam shell brain popped open again and the creature closed its big, ugly eye.

The brain-butt seeped mucous from its creases.

I could not help but cringe.

'Yes,' Grāf said calmly. 'I am causing those sensations.' At least it was direct, I thought. Pulses thumped through the trees again: thumped through my chest. It was a wave of influence that carried suggestive emotional energy, and an urge to comply fell over me like a heavy quilt.

"Stop whatever it is you're doing," I commanded. I tried to sound polite but self-assured, but it came out shakier than I'd intended. The being stopped its slow, skittering approach.

"Has it been you this whole time," I asked.

'How do you mean,' the thing thought. The pulsating stopped as it asked the question.

"I've been out here and felt that... thumping – or – or pulsing before," I said plainly. "You're trying to influence me somehow. I have felt urges against my own free will. Urges to stay or go and sit or run off in a panic. Stop that; I would prefer to be equals. If we understand each other, I'd much rather talk than absorb your influence." Sometimes, I just found the right words for the job... even if they were slurred with drink.

'I apologize.'

"So, you admit it?" Even as I challenged it, I felt inclined to befriend the strange sentient thing.

'Yes, I admit it,' Grāf said plainly, 'I was trying to keep you away from my campsite. It is best that I avoid interacting with potential sentients here.'

As our commune reached this treaty, there flashed before my mind's eye impressions of Grāf's life cycle. I had the strong sense by now that the stranger was biologically nongender – I could feel from its experiences that it was capable of parthenogenesis. Emotional attachment to one parent, and emotional attachment to two clutches of little ones, still pink with soft, undeveloped carapaces, flashed before me. But never was there a hint of a second parent or of any partners.

From my mind's attempt to define this, I also had an immediate sense that concepts of sexual reproduction were foreign to it – something it had been fascinated to understand as a result of my personal lamentations on human social structures. As a result of this realization coupled with Grāf's clearly demonstrated sentience, I must correct my own xenophobic thinking and here cease to use 'it' as Grāf's pronoun, for 'they' were easily an intellectual equal.

"How do you do it... that sensation?" I wanted to know what I was up against. Perhaps they had a device. If so, perhaps I could use it against them... should I need to. I was unsure if they were a threat.

'It is a natural trait of my kind,' they thought calmly. 'But you wouldn't know that... we are the first of our species to encounter each other,' the blue crab concluded cheerfully, blinking their big eye meaningfully at me.

"You came through there," I asked, pointing at the doorway-shaped jelly membrane. It was a guess.

'Through there, yes.' they thought, and pointed at the doorway again, as if to dispel any possible confusion.

I heard the trickle of the creek nearby.

My mind was still racing.

Gräf.

"I am called Gerald," I said, "I am what is called a *homo sapiens...*" I trailed off, then found my way again. "...and you are on planet Earth." Hadn't shared that yet, either.

This was first contact, de Vere! Stay sharp!

"What do your people call themselves," I asked, realizing that, in my overwhelmed state, I had not yet inquired.

They closed their massive eye, rocked low on all eight of their claws, and sighed. I was overtaken by visions of Gräf's home world — of dome-like mounds stacked up along a shoreline — muddy mint sand packed thick as it hugged a great sea of amber yellow liquid. Jagged wedges of shiny black barnacles dotted the ocean's horizon, jutting from its surface like watchtowers of broken glass.

Trusting by now that Gräf was not going to harm me, I closed my eyes. Still the images came, but I could see them clearer without the influence of my physical sight. 'Home,' the words finally formed, perhaps because Gräf was unsure how to translate them. 'You may call my kind the *Plurespedes*,' they said, perhaps drawing on my own limited knowledge of Latin? I could no longer be sure, particularly given that Gräf had already admitted to learning about Earth by reading my thoughts.

'Home is the Gurrrd,' Gräf purred the 'R' sound, and I

95

heard their chelicera click even as they thought the word.

My mind was breaking. I'd always wanted something like this to happen – always hoped I'd confirm my suspicions about the universe beyond – but when confronted with it, especially all at once, I felt walls collapsing between my ears.

Back my spirit went from me,
Away and out-of-body.
Groped my soul as conscience fled,
Numb, my brain wished I were dead.
Brash and bold are clownish apes,
For ignoring nature's fate.
We toil all our time away,
Making fun and making play.
No one lives on past their day,
Without giving Death his say...

Never getting very far,
Never mind how small we are.
Never looking up ahead,
Always egos seeing red.

Ashes to ashes,
Dust to dust,
Human nature
Should be cussed.

Thoughts galloped off in stampede; I either missed them or merely caught their silhouettes as they rushed past. My brain was keeping only what it needed to survive. I stood by, comprehending. My mind watched my soul, regarding it like a wad of gum trying to reunite a car tire with asphalt in the hot summer sun. With a deep breath, I backed the car up to relieve the stress on my gummy soul.

Stick to observations: keep it basic.

"The goo I see in the doorway and, uh, on your…" I trailed off.

'My brain," it said, waggling its butt-shell again.

"Yeah…" I uttered slowly. "I saw that floating down stream two days ago."

'Yes,' Grāf nodded. 'It's a reaction to the atmosphere on this side of the barrier. Organic material from my world seems to react by producing extra secretion. I suspect it's the lack of fresh air I've detected here. It's thinner, and tastes of decay. The difference causes my stress coat to cycle,' Grāf's voice cackled awkwardly in my head like I'd missed a fart joke.

More slime oozed from Grāf's creases. 'So far as I can tell,' they went on, 'these secretions do not negatively affect wildlife here… though I am afraid I upset a few frogs… but I took them to a safe alternative not far from here.'

I stared into their bulbous yellow eye, mesmerized as they blinked slowly. My mind dug its claws into the intellectual dirt. Where were the strings? The hidden puppeteer? I never watched TV anymore; perhaps there was some prank reality show on SciFi featuring cryptids. I peered under Grāf's shell — no appendages, no illusions I could detect.

They clicked their mouth again.

'I must build a fire,' they thought, then clamped their shell shut and danced delicately over to a pile of branches and tree bark which seemed to have been stacked there for some time. How spider-like, I realized. Perhaps that's what my mind was doing. Yes, that was it! I'd been in the woods studying the spiders… in the *heat*, no less… and my in-laws had ocean décor throughout the house, *including* a blue metal crab that sat and stared at me whilst I was on the pot. Yes, of course!

This was certainly all conjured in my brain somehow. I was sure of it. The creature before me struck flint and lit a little fire, revealing more of themselves. I could see just how thick with mucous their joints were. Had my mind conjured allergies for this fictional phantom?

Suddenly, in most disgusting fashion, Grāf came to a sudden halt, dropped the wood they were carrying, and sneezed. It was not, however, the typical sneeze an Earthling might imagine. No, no! Picture, if you will, a blue crab the size of a small hedge expelling a gust of air and mucous from every crease and crevice between their crusty limbs. Those globs of slime spattered and slapped across my face.

The texture alone was enough to make me sick: wet and heavy like a massive glob of hair gel. But it was the stank that did me in; a putrid combination of copper, peppermint and fish oil that knocked me backwards. I retched twice, then vomited on Grāf's newborn fire.

Like a well-timed transition for the stage, the woods shifted into blackout because of my blunder, and so too, did my mind.

10. WORLDS APART

'How do you feel?' Grāf's mind asked gently. Dizzy – I felt dizzy. I had three separate headaches all at once… a migraine, sore temples, and a pinch at the base of my skull. All that, and yet my lips and cheeks were numb.

Grāf's small fire was still crackling. It was keeping me warm.

Extending a claw, my strange new friend offered me a metal flagon of water. 'Here,' they said, 'I have boiled and purified water from your stream. It would help to drink it, particularly if you are still feeling faint.'

Shadows from mighty trees danced around the little fire.

Grāf's big, yellow, ungodly eye blinked at me.

Mucous gathered in globs around the edges of that toxic orb, green veins thumping as the strange diamond pupil expanded and contracted at me.

Surely, I was mad by now… and yet, there was Grāf, standing in front of me, swaying on six of their eight legs.

"I need to sit," I finally said, asking no forgiveness for it. Reality was confronting me in waves, the alcohol was nervously rocking the ship and making things worse.

'I understand,' the being nodded... or rather, it bowed, closing its eye, and breaking that unsettling visual contact. 'I have had far more time to process your existence. I imagine it will take you some time... as it did me.'

Damn them for being so nice. How dare they make me feel comfortable while these crushing epiphanies swept over me.

"Why are you here," I prodded.

'Curiosity,' they said, lifting their two foremost left claws and pointing at the strange gooey rectangle in the tree trunk. 'I found that portal and decided to go through. It connects our worlds.'

"Wait, so you're just back and forth through here daily," I asked, nodding at the strange gelatinous portal. Bubbles rolled in its plasma like goo in a lava lamp.

'No, no,' Grāf shook their head. 'I must not return until I have gathered as many of your world's details as possible, for I do not know how many times I may pass through there. I have not been back home.'

I watched Grāf under the moonlight, looking for the seams. Waiting to see the hand of the puppeteer extended up out of the Plurespedes' clamshell butt. No dosage of Winston or Henson could have prepared me for the nature of Grāf.

They saw me reach out a hand as if to slow the spinning of the globe. Smiling, they waited silently until I had regained my composure.

"How is your world compared to this one," I asked. I took a generous swig of the water and worked it around in my mouth. I was trying to rinse out the sour tang of stale tequila and lime.

The yarn that Grāf spun in my mind next was such that I can only paraphrase. Their people, the Plurespedes, were a species that thrived along the shores of their great planet. These eight-legged beings were not far advanced in the ways of science, for they were trapped in a vicious life cycle that kept them working on the pale green sands. All day, they'd burrow through the wet sands for food and shelter. It was crucial to their life cycle, and yet, each night the vicious lemon sea swept their sandy burrows and towers away. In the morning, when the tide pulled out, the Plurespedes began their daily ritual of digging for their dinner and their shelter.

And they covered their beaches in the thousands, gossiping the day away with social banter across the pock-marked sands. It sounded as if some philosophy and problem solving were entering into their culture, as they were able to telepathically link: a hive mind to plot their shoreline work more efficiently.

But Grāf was just a curious young crab who'd crawled through a wormhole, not some grand explorer with the mind of a great scientist. Just another social recluse with an interest in the natural world.

In that way, we were kindred spirits.

I felt no safer from the violent churnings of Earth's whirling forces than an ant building its hill in a suburbanite's backyard. My life meant very little in the grand scheme. That was a realization that would further scratch my already melancholy lens. I doubted I'd feel differently a year or two or more from that very instant, because in that instant I realized how trivial I was.

I explained these thoughts to Grāf... explained that, from my perspective, so many of my species were propelled by ego alone... trapped in materialistic routines and rituals – even the disagreements bandied about that year were all arguments over whether or not to 'keep the world going.' When it stopped, so many people realized how unsatisfied they really were... at least, those lucky enough to live to that point. But already, that social self-awareness was waning again.

I wanted someone to teach us a lesson... we certainly didn't seem to be learning any for ourselves. As a kid, I always thought it would take an alien species to unite humankind's efforts. If they seemed more advanced, all the better.

Gräf fell silent, so I just stared as they used a pair of claws to rub mucous from their wide and furious oculus. My mind wandered into a wave of sublime euphoria. I was the first human to encounter a Plurespedes. How might I claim such historic significance?

Anxiety stirred in the pit of my stomach, loosing rabid butterflies. Without proof, who would believe me? I was nothing special: a collection of particles, all infinitesimally divisible, all dismissible as 'dust in the wind.' The dust and the wind whistled between my waking mind and my infernal, everlasting soul.

A heap of shit is handed down...
Upon inspection no way 'round,
So, wallow through those boggy mounds,
Where human nature's soaked the ground.

The vile muck of egos past,
Enlightened here, it cannot last.
Onward plow into that shit,
The sins of man have all been writ!
Up they grapple, unto death
Where even still, they cannot rest.

Why rest?
Why wait?
Why consternate?
Why must we blindly masticate?

'Because, dear boy,' some will reply,
'You've too much idol in thine eye.'
There's no denying human fate
Would rather sit and masturbate.

"Are you okay," Grāf asked, shaking me from my spiraling thoughts.

"Yeah," I lied, waving it all away. My brain felt sore as it stopped rumbling. I clasped the bridge of my nose with my fingers.

Grāf fell silent, allowing me to have the moment. Silence, though not my strong suit, was that night found to be just as informing as conversation, and the silence that fell over us at the campsite next indicated to me that our time would not last much longer.

The fire crackled and the trees swayed in a gentle breeze. My friends the frogs croaked in sync, keeping rhythm with one another. The sky was still clear, and I'd finally forgotten about Death. That was a first, and one that made me grateful for Grāf's presence.

We talked about human social structures. I shared observations of how cities tended to have their own pulse – one that either satisfied high-achievers or helped them to burn out early in life. It was reminiscent of how my collaborators spoke fondly of unveiling Manhattan's treasures, though all I ever uncovered was utter chaos.

Scrambling to keep my head above water – hell, to get it above water in the first place – had been as violent as the thrashing of a drowning child. I didn't mention that my lack of financial means most often boycotted my path to artistic notoriety, for I hadn't the resources of those I was up against. I had passion and a modicum of talent, but they were lofty goods in a land bereft of meritocracy.

It mocked me at every turn.

Why mention it then and there?

My woes were not for Grāf's fine ear; the more our conversation tarried near them, the more I felt like I was painting myself to be a failure with a struggling psyche. We two were worlds apart in every way, yet we were building understanding.

We laughed together at biological questions. Grāf shared with me that the Plurespedes lived for approximately fifty of the Gurrrd's years, were mature after only two, and were able to reproduce after about five.

"That is hard for me to imagine," I admitted.

'It is hard for me to imagine reproduction as I have witnessed here. This requirement for coupling seems… inconvenient.' I entertained their questions on the matter, explained what I could, and ultimately, we landed on its cultural role among my species.

"Humans have constructed such negative stigmas around the act. Shame was instilled in ancient cultures as a form of population control and intertwined into theology to be more efficacious. We've come to realize all these things, and yet our cultures still carry the stigmas proudly, like they would a veteran's scars."

This led us to deeper, darker parts of my psyche. Succinctly, I explained to them that I had witnessed the beautiful creation my species was capable of… but that those feats were vastly outnumbered by the self-indulgent, self-sanctimonious venom of our egos. I was in a social tailspin, but I'd torn the Band-Aid off, so I kept going in spite of myself.

"There's a saying," I shared, "derived from a statement by the scientist Max Planck: 'Science advances one funeral at a time.' I've always felt that, with humans, the saying could pertain to all of my species: 'Progress happens one funeral at a time.' What do you think?"

'I think you're not very fond of your own kind,' Grāf did not blink when they stated it. I would not hide my broken self from this keen observer.

"No," I said weakly, "I'm not even a fan of myself, really." It was only fair to everyone else. "I mean, I try to be a good person – at least, I think I do – but I'm coming unraveled more each day. I can't be nice anymore. I'm tired of watching people blissfully destroy the natural world. There's no value in anything outside of the Terran 'self.' And I see it and think, 'Christ, if this is me and I'm really trying, where the fuck is everyone else headed?' It makes me hopeless... hopeless for the other life around me. We don't take any of them into consideration."

Grāf bobbled, rocking on their legs, as if nodding in understanding. 'The Plurespedes have a saying: "Pop your head above the sand as oft you can, for you need a clear view of the stars above to navigate the shores below." Your people could benefit from such advice.'

The fire died, sputtering a few final embers, and I turned back to the southeast, toward the tree line that marked my new neighborhood. The sun – Sol – was gathering its skirts of light just over the horizon.

"I need to get home," I said reluctantly. "My family's bound to wake up and wonder why I'm not around."

Grāf nodded. 'It's been my pleasure,' they said.

"As well as mine," I confirmed with a smile. "And I think I shall sleep well having had this talk."

I showed them how to shake hands – or claws – and then I turned my attention to the trees again, following the faint light of daybreak.

11. NEIGHBORS

Part of me wishes I had wandered right home, but perhaps if I had, I wouldn't have as much story to tell. With my head full of clamshell brain-butts and clicking claws, I miscalculated. It was fate that I should, for I stumbled headlong into a most detestable scenario.

As morning gripped the night sky's throat, I found myself one cul-de-sac north of my destination. Before popping out of the underbrush, I had crouched down, stopping to check my surroundings. I didn't want to be seen exiting the woods before 6 AM; it would rouse all kinds of suspicion. It was a good thing I hesitated, for just as I was about to stand, seeing that the coast was clear, the headlights of a beat-up Jeep Cherokee washed over my face. The vehicle rounded the corner onto that street. The beams of light swung over the wet pavement as the Jeep veered to the last house on my left and parked perpendicularly across its one-car driveway. The choice didn't seem peculiar at first, since there was a Toyota sedan already parked in the driveway at 126 Slate Drive.

The Jeep was an old one, with a chassis that rattled while the engine was running and patches of rust across the wheel wells that had eaten away at the flaking gold paint job. Its old motor choked before it cut out, and the driver side door swung open. My breath caught in my chest as I identified that wild white hair; it was Jim.

Thank God I hadn't plunged out of the woods as he was coming up the street, I thought. After writing it all down, I was convinced he had come out on his ATV a few nights prior just to scare me away – probably didn't like the rattling of my skateboard on the pavement.

I decided to wait until he was out of sight, then I'd move back into the woods. If I moved and he saw me, he might be wild enough to rush in after me.

So, I waited. Then the wild-haired man did something strange... he locked his Jeep and walked across the lawn up to the house next door – 124 Slate Drive. As he did so, the front door at 124 opened, and another man, unmistakable in girth, greeted him.

Butch.

He stood in the doorway, that hulking silhouette who could only be described as fat. The screen door swung wide, and they both disappeared inside.

No sooner had they closed the door when the garage opened over at 126. A young black man, perhaps just a few years older than me, emerged with a briefcase in-hand.

"Oh, God damnit," he muttered softly as he unlocked his own car – the Toyota that was now blocked in by Jim's rugged old Jeep. "Again, with this shit?" He tossed his briefcase in the back seat as a preteen girl ran out of the garage, stopping to reach inside and press the door controls so the garage closed behind her. I noted her backpack and lunchbox; she was clearly headed into school. But not if it wasn't even six yet, I reasoned. Maybe it was later in the morning than I thought. But the streetlights were still on, and the sky was that strange, deep blue of a looming dreary day.

Just then, the girl saw the ugly old Jeep at the end of their driveway. Her shoulders dropped as she shook her head. "We're gonna' be late again," she complained. "Why do they always do this?"

"We're not gonna' be late. Just wait for me in the car," her dad said reassuringly. He dropped his keys, and I was able to see his face more clearly – he bore a striking resemblance to a young Joe Morton, the actor I knew best as Miles Dyson in James Cameron's *Terminator 2*. This instantly endeared me to him, for I had always been empathetic to that tragic character. I made note of the similarities as he marched up the sidewalk to his neighbors at 124 and rang the doorbell.

He straightened up his back as the shadows of the two men inside stretched out across the foyer. Butch the fat man opened the door, his expression blank. His tiny mole eyes blinked indignantly.

"What," Butch said bluntly after a long beat. It was a challenge, not a query.

"I already asked you not to let Jim park across my driveway," the young man said.

"Jim's his own person," Butch belched back.

"When he's over here, he's your guest. He should park in your driveway."

"There's no room," Butch said with a shrug. The young dad glanced over his shoulder: the fat man's driveway was only one car wide, but there were no cars parked in it at all.

"How do you figure that?"

"Look here, Ray," Jim's weaselly voice cackled from inside the house. Jim's wild white hair slipped into the doorway, standing between Butch and Ray from 126. "I already told you last time – if I park in Butch's driveway, then he can't get the truck outta' the garage when we leave for work." His neck trembled and his face turned even redder than usual – he was locked in confrontation, and his dark eyebrows jiggled as he tamped down his anger.

"Just park on the street and pull in when you're leaving,"

Ray reasoned as politely as he could. "When you block me in, it makes us both late," he added, gesturing to his daughter in the front seat.

"Y'know, I'm already tired of you being on Butch's private property," Jim sneered.

"Jim," Butch warned, clearly trying to play nice.

"Oh, yeah," Ray retorted, "isn't that ironic?"

"I think it's time you git," Jim spat back. Forget micro-aggressions, I thought. Jim was straight up nasty. There was something animalistic in the way his chest heaved, and the way he kept his mouth open like a wolf baring its teeth. I remembered his ATV antics – recalled the shotgun scabbard he'd been wearing, and I shivered. Had Ray seen that, he might not be so bold now, I thought. As I watched his body language, I grew convinced Jim had the devil in him; there was no telling what he might do... or to whom.

Butch shifted, displaying mild signs of awkwardness.

"Jim," Ray said, ignoring Butch's squirming, "are you going to move your Jeep?"

"I don't see why I should," wiry Jim said as he worked his fingers through his wild white mane.

Ray laughed in surprise. "Is that how it is," he asked.

"That's how it is," Jim confirmed with a nod.

"Okay," Ray said, "but I'm calling the Homeowners' Association about this. Don't say I didn't try to talk first either, 'cause that's what this is. Could've just been nothing; a friendly conversation man-to-man." He popped his chest out slightly as he back-pedaled down his neighbor's lawn.

I couldn't help but roll my eyes. 'Man-to-man' was worthless. It had never gotten me anywhere but into heated confrontations with strangers – usually older men whose egos bruised like Georgia peaches when someone told them they were wrong. Just another bullshit double-standard.

"Jim," Butch sighed, "move yer Jeep."

"What?" Jim seemed surprised.

"I don't want no trouble," Butch said. "Go make nice with my neighbor and move yer goddamned Jeep." Butch didn't make eye contact with his friend, he just stared straight ahead, shooting daggers into the back of Ray's head with his angry, steer-like gaze. He held his screen door open.

Jim shook his head, obliging his large friend's 'request,' the wind whipping up his hair as he stepped away from the house. Butch watched as Jim backed his Jeep up, and Ray waved in thanks as he drove away. Jim didn't acknowledge it, just sulked. His pouting cheeks reminded me of a kid from school who'd been the classroom dunce. He never thought his punishments were deserved. I cringed as I remembered that Chuckie Doll come-to-life, with his liar's dimples, thick lashes, and angry freckles. Satan's little Howdy-Doody, I used to call him.

I shook off the memory. Jim struck me as fitting the dunce demographic. As he parked his Jeep at the end of the street, close to the trees, Butch hobbled out to join him. He wore crocs, basketball shorts and a tank top. His pale little face was shrouded under a UNC ballcap, for he was so fair skinned that I swear I witnessed the folds on the back of his neck burning pink even in the early morning light. As he approached, I saw that Butch's whole face was small for his fat head, and his nose came to a point like a rat's.

I was suddenly hyper-aware of my own face, which contorted with disgust as I heard Jim mutter the N-word. These men had just proven to be even uglier on the inside, and my skin crawled as they got closer.

"He's got it coming," Jim said.

"You think so," Butch asked rhetorically.

"I know so," Jim responded with conviction.

"Young people are entitled these days. They don't got respect for their elders," Butch observed.

"Sometimes, I wanna' teach 'em some myself..." Jim trailed off. I swore I could hear the gears in his head creaking as they attempted to turn.

Overhead, two small shadows shrieked and clashed, squabbling in the sky together... bats. They careened out of the forest and into the roof-peaked open sky of suburbia. The change in surroundings did not seem to faze them. Instead, they continued on their chaotic trajectory, wings beating each other senseless.

"Can we watch the game here tonight," Jim asked.

"Maybe," Butch said, "I don't like the preseason junk."

"Barb's outta' town," Jim reminded him. "We can order wings... my treat?"

I saw Butch's ears prick like a dog who'd just heard the word, 'treat.' He reconsidered, letting a big dumb grin overtake his chubby cheeks. "Okay," he said at last.

Out west, thunder rumbled over the forest. To the north, behind Butch's house, two bolts of the most molten red lightning I have ever seen ruptured the pillowing storm clouds. I didn't know lightning was capable of such colors, but there it was, stunning the sky overhead for a few fleeting seconds.

"Yeah," Jim went on, "and if we get bored, we should go see your neighbor." He winked.

"Jeez, Jim... seriously?"

"If the opportunity knocks, we should take it."

"Shoot," Butch said, "you sound just like my grandad. We gotta' be careful talkin' like that; someone's liable to find us out."

"With the way things are, now's the time to do it," Jim said smugly. "People waking up to the truth of things all over this country. Almost every day, a {redacted} goes missing. Cops're more likely to think it was some stranger on the way home from work. Plus, with riots all over, they got better things to do."

"Sounds like you've given this a lot of thought," Butch said. I couldn't tell if he was put off by Jim's confession or not.

"What's that supposed to mean?"

"I just didn't know you, uh, took those kinda' risks."

"It ain't that risky. There's been a bunch of stories in the news about young guys like Ray. Like that kid who 'hung' himself out in Los Angeles. Even big city cops called that a suicide." Jim stopped, scanning the street for neighbors. "C'mon," he said, "let's grab our coffee and git'. I don't wanna' be talking about this outside no more."

They trudged back up to 124 and as soon as their shadows moved away from Butch's front door, I reached for my phone. I fumbled, snapping zoomed in photos of Jim's license plate. I'd wait long enough to get a photo of Butch's plate, too, then I would turn my story in to...

Who?

Would the cops down here take my report seriously?

My mind reeled and my stomach boiled acid in its empty pit as I thought it through.

Deep in thought, I jumped out of my skin when Butch's garage door squealed, lurching open. Jim and he rolled down the driveway in that familiar pearly diesel-sucking pick-up. Sunglasses on and country music cranked, they rolled out like the Hillbilly Blues Brothers...

Fat Man and Little Boy, out to spread their toxic waste.

A caricature of Americana.

Foolishness.

What the hell was I going to do?

I backpedaled carefully into the woods, retracing the tree line until I was on my own street.

12. PIECE OF CAKE

Before I stepped out of the woods and onto the lawn, a car radio gave me pause. Staying back, I ducked behind a tree. I peered hard at the headlights coming up Redstone drive, trying to discern what type of vehicle they belonged to. I saw only a pearly white glow.

Then I recognized the country song...

The fat ass chrome grill and the longhorn-style rearview mirrors...

It was Butch and Jim. They rumbled up to a spot two houses down and parked right on the lawn. Then, after an embarrassingly long interim, I had the most frightful realization: Butch was commuting a block to work by motor vehicle rather than just taking a walk. He was *that breed* of languid. There was no reasoning with men like that.

I slipped up the side yard.

Buzz, buzz, thump.

Buzz, buzz, thump.

The front porch light was on – had been all night – and the same cicada was beating itself senseless as it tried to fly into its luminance.

Death was in the shadows of that dumb cicada's actions. Quietly, I eased through the back door, chugged twenty-eight ounces of water, and gently lighted the stairs. I heard my fiancé stir and so ducked into the bathroom. Quickly, I went through the motions of a morning shower, then slipped into bed.

I decided I should rest before I could think straight about a remedy for the madness I had overheard. I shut my eyes and plunged my thoughts into raging waters, trying to drown them in a sea of sleep.

As I lay racing through my thoughts,
I shuddered on my sleeping cot
To think a creature with eight legs,
Had visited this drunken dreg.
Had we, in truth, really communed,
Or was Gräf trauma well-costumed?

What of the thumping in my chest
Might it to someone soon suggest
That all I saw and heard of Gräf
Was worthy only of vouchsafe.
Plurespedes: blue crab spider,
Did I dream of that outsider?

Next onto racists my mind stepped,
Since that exchange I could accept.
Should I suppress this ugly doubt,
And go and call those bastards out?
For that, at least, I knew was true,
And for those hicks, my anger grew.

I would not let them both succeed,
And I ignored my darker need,
To tear those pests out by the root.
I drifted off, thus resolute:

If they touched Ray, I'd intervene,
To cause them re'grets quite obscene.

ᛣ   ᛤ

Four hours later, I awoke to the smell of fresh coffee and pancakes. The family had all slept in and were making a concerted effort to start the day right rather than feeling shame about rising late.

In the restroom, I locked eyes with the metal crab and my conundrum came rushing back to me. The explorer Grāf felt even more distant now, as foggy a memory as if the whole encounter had happened years ago. I had had no chance to consider it further once the morning unfolded. Was it all in my head? The way anxiety beat in my chest told me it had been real. The sinking, sickening, dipping, diving flutter that gripped my insides told me I was still grappling with existence somewhere in my subconscious… that I didn't want to believe it, but that Grāf had been undeniably real.

For a short time, I escaped my concerns, choosing to focus instead on the elements of the present. The scent of maple and melted butter, the sweet baking batter stinging the air, and the smell of the fresh coffee overwhelmed my fears in a cloud of comforts. But that evil lurked in the shadows of my consciousness, less than fifty feet away, across a few lawns.

What was I to do?

I thought of Grāf – would they understand enough to be able to help me?

Could I find them again, explain my need for help, and make it back to Slate Drive in time to intervene?

I had to try.

Those rednecks had alerted me to their disease by speaking their horrible ignorance out loud.

Diseased. That's what they were. If I attempted to intervene – to help Ray – it would have to get physical. I would need weapons to defend myself, and I needed to be ready to hurt someone.

Was I prepared for that?

What did that even mean?

I posed those questions to myself as I loaded up the dishwasher, a strangely domestic juxtaposition to the maelstrom in my mind.

Then I realized it was Monday.

Despite my deepest wishes, I had not been laid off work during the pandemic. Instead, I had been plugging away at my soul-sucking IT job, one that had gotten markedly better once I didn't have to see anyone in person. Everyone had finally stopped calling when they had little issues. Instead, they were finally resorting to Google to avoid human contact, as was becoming human custom.

It was fine; allowed me to focus on my own goals and projects – to sit and enjoy the lack of supervision usually afforded to anyone in office who looked like they were under the age of thirty. Though I was not, I was often crammed into that category. It was complimentary, save for a heavy dose of agist condescension.

The day dragged by.

Around 2:00 pm Eastern, I unplugged from work. If someone needed me, they'd call my cell. No sense sitting in the recycled air conditioning while I sweated away the hours trying to formulate a plan of defense.

I sat at the back window and watched Butch and Jim raising the neighbor's wooden monstrosity over the pond.

Were those dip-shits serious?

I was worried that my need to even ask was, in fact, my answer. The way Jim talked indicated a pattern of premeditated harm to Butch's neighbor. I didn't think he was just blowing off steam. I'd be a fool to do so.

Based on the last few days, I figured they would both be back at 124 Slate Drive around seven, which meant I needed an excuse to miss dinner. Perhaps it could be a night for fending – the family had agreed that some nights would not include a planned meal for everyone. This was fine, as I hadn't expected such doting when we agreed to abscond down south.

Because my mind kept flitting from idea to idea all day, I decided to focus on one challenge at a time. First was getting clear for the dinner hour. I floated the idea of having leftovers to my fiancé, who was glad at the idea of something easy. The proposition sat well with her mother, too.

Step one complete.

Step two: wardrobe. I needed clothes that would camouflage me while also protecting me from the elements. I had black pants and an olive-green Henley, so that would be my base, with a black hoodie over it. I pulled dark blue socks – they were long enough to tuck my pant legs down into, so I was less likely to get a critter crawling around in my shoe or, worse yet, up my leg.

It was important to cover my face so I couldn't be identified. I had nothing but a beanie-style knit cap. It was dark, but it wouldn't cover my face. In movies, I always saw people wearing pantihose over their faces.

Oh! My mother-in-law had just been showing me a sewing project she was doing that had required a pack of black pantihose. We'd been talking about puppet materials and techniques. She had joked about me using them for a costume, as I was known to go all-out for my character getups.

I waited until my fiancé ducked into the restroom and slipped around the corner into the sewing room. There was the packet, still stuffed with articles of hosiery. Grabbing just one, I was careful not to make a mess of anything else sitting out. I stuffed it in my pocket as I heard the bathroom door open.

Step two complete.

Step three: armaments. Certainly, one of those Draconian Quagmires had a firearm that would be joining their dark deed. I had nothing that would stop a bullet, nor did I have anything with which to fire back. But I needed to have something with which to disarm and fend them off. My thinking was to observe from a distance until the opportunity to intervene presented itself. And to avoid conflict if they failed, I would wait until it was clear that intervention was necessary. The goons had to go after Ray first. My suspicion was that Jim intended to use the woods, which made my intervention feasible. The close quarters would be far better for melee combat, and like the farmers of feudal Japan hundreds of years ago, my only defense was a set of gardening tools.

I swallowed the lump in my throat. It had been pressing against my Adam's Apple all morning like a forceful thumb and as my planning continued, it tightened into a fist, threatening to force my breakfast up.

There was a hatchet in the little tool cupboard out back, I remembered. Come to think of it, I may have used a pickaxe to help with yard work the last time I visited. Everyone was bustling about with chores, so I waited until things settled and everyone retreated upstairs, as was often their habit.

I should clarify: the tool cupboard was technically one of those free-standing plastic things I called 'Playskool for Adults.' The hatchet was hanging on the left as soon as I opened the door. The blade was bigger than I'd remembered.

Hefting it in my hand, I decided to snag a pair of rubber gardening gloves, too. As I leaned in to grab them, I spotted the pickaxe buried in the far-right corner under a rake and three shovels. Tucking the hatchet under the charcoal grill, I checked my surroundings to make sure no one had come downstairs.

Next, I scanned the neighbors' yards that sprawled south, over my right shoulder. I didn't want a soul to see me, least of all Butch and Jim. They were down by the water, their backs to me as they drove nails into the deck they were erecting.

What did I think I was going to do? These tools could easily kill someone.

Was I willing to go that far?

No.

Definitely not, I told myself... unless in self-defense or in the defense of an innocent. Though, I didn't know if that held up in a court of law.

I watched the sun beat down on Butch's pink neck folds.

I saw Jim scowl at one of the other workers.

My blood ran hot as I watched them, thinking of all they'd said... I decided I did want to hurt them. Perhaps the anger made me excited at the chance to beat a lesson into one of them. I had no desire to take a life – even if I did think they were a waste of carbon better suited for sod.

Enjoy your day, you rotten pigs,
While I hide weapons in the twigs.
Your judgement will soon be at hand,
And if you harm your fellow man,
I'll beat you senseless, feed you steel,
And overcome your inbred zeal.

A forceful breeze stirred the leafy branches all around, and the distant groan of a train whistle drifted to me on the wind. I was staring at them. Fortunately, their backs were to me. The only movement was Jim reaching for the water jug.

I averted my eyes and tamped down my hate.

All clear.

Gently, I pulled the shovels out one at a time. The first two came out with no problem, but as I wrapped my hand around the third shovel, a rake fell forward, clattering to the ground. I froze, unwilling to even cuss at myself. Suddenly, I understood how rabbits felt when they had been spotted by a dog. Adrenaline charged into my chest and sent my heart aflutter, but I breathed through it and waited a few beats. No activity in the backyards.

Down on the deck, Butch huffed and switched on the radio. Apart from that, there was no reaction. No new noises, and all was unchanged inside my home.

Shaking my head, I crouched down. Instead of grabbing the rake handle and pulling the thing out, I reached down and lifted the forks first, being sure to work them slowly away from the other tools they threatened to ensnare. Next, I procured the pickaxe, slid it under the grill, and put the other tools back as quickly and quietly as I could manage. The trick, I reminded myself, was fluid and controlled movement. It was also my trick for sneaking around quietly when others I lived with were slumbering.

After trying my luck with the tool shed ruckus, I thought it best to put the keys back inside first. In truth, that was so I could check to make sure no one inside was curious about the sound. Finding that the coast was clear, I hooked the keys in their spot and went back outside.

Still no neighbors in their yards – that was good. I grabbed my chosen defenses and slid slyly down the sloping side yard. Into the trees I went, feeling better with each leafy arm my barky friends extended between me and the neighborhood. There was a stack of boulders just beyond the property, where the woods met the pond. I slid the tools under one these, in a space that was open on both ends.

Step three complete.

My deed done, I slipped the rubber gardening gloves in my pocket and climbed the hill back up to the house. Fatigue draped itself over me like one of those lead aprons at the dentist's office, and I was instantly aware of how heavy my head felt on my shoulders.

Right, I realized. I had lost an entire night's sleep after drinking far too much alcohol. As the throbbing pain at the base of my skull grew worse, I tried stretching out my neck. This was either dehydration or a side effect of the stress gripping my body. Even though I suspected the latter, I returned home, filled a water bottle, and chugged it down.

The two-hour nap I had managed that morning upon my

return was not going to cut it. I needed to be able to stay up late again to deal with those buffoons. It was about eleven-thirty, and the sun was bright that day, so I drew the shades and set an alarm for six, then gave my fiancé a kiss and explained that I hadn't slept well. Then, I retreated to bed where I nursed another water until I nodded off to sleep.

My dreams were clouded – no people, no animals – just the sound of a breeze rustling unseen trees and a strange, pulsing river of light. The colors ebbed and flowed just beneath the water like an RGB display fluxing inside a computer. The river dragged me downstream as a full spectrum of colors danced around me. It was thick, like syrup, but it was easy.

It soothed me.

I tried to let go.

'Psychedelic molasses,' a far-off voice said with a reassuring laugh.

Maybe it was Grāf?

Grāf, the Plurespedes from the Gurrrd.

It struck me as sounding like something I might make up for a science fiction farce. That was just denial; there was no suppressing the authenticity of my experience. The human mind would always resist such drastic shifts in perspective to preserve the ego.

The only way to know was to find the campsite again.

I could go back, I told myself, but I had to get through the night. I had to solve the Butch and Jim issue first. Putting concerns of my own psyche to bed was of secondary importance; someone's safety was at risk...

☙　　　❧

I drifted in a lazy river of day sleep until the jarring chime of my alarm startled me back to consciousness with an instant migraine. In New York, afternoon naps left me feeling thick in the head, like a half-assed hangover. In more recent years, I took it as a sign of aging and tried avoiding naps altogether.

This one might actually be part hangover.

Lying there for a few quiet moments, I rubbed the bridge of my nose to coax the pain out. The bedroom door squeaked open just a crack and my fiancé smiled in at me.

"Oh, good," she said, "you're awake."

"Just barely," I mumbled with a grin. "I've got a headache."

"Dinner's ready – you probably need food." Fuck, I thought I'd taken care of that. Knowing that I was prone to doze off again, my fiancé waited in the doorway for me to get up. She didn't realize I couldn't afford to. I swung my legs over the side of the bed and stood slowly.

"Weren't we going to do our own thing," I asked, trying to sound innocent. I knew that, if I shared my plans with her, she'd try to stop me – not because what I was doing was wrong, but because she'd be concerned for my safety.

"Yeah, but my dad had his heart set on spaghetti, and it didn't take us long to whip it up."

"Oh," I said, trying to sound pleased.

Dinner was spent in a fog as I struggled to keep my nerves at bay, eating quickly but trying not to look like I was rushing. When anxiety kicked up, it often took hold of my throat, squeezing my gag reflex while my stomach did somersaults.

I must've refilled my water a dozen times, gulping it down to placate the clenching in my throat. Luckily, we were all done eating in about twenty minutes. I was sure not to rush conversation and my father-in-law helped with cleanup, so all was said and done in about thirty-five minutes. Even with a belly full of food, my head still hurt. And, despite all the water, my mouth felt dry and tacky, like the alcohol still coated it. If not for the shower I'd managed earlier, I had no doubt I'd have stunk like liquor sweats all day, too.

"What's everyone's evening looking like," my mother-in-law asked the room. "I was thinking maybe we could do a movie night?"

Shit.

"I need to work on my video for Dreamscapes," my fiancé chimed in as I was fishing for my own excuse. During quarantine, she'd been making extra money on the side by shooting little promo videos of the country's newest hobby, Diamond Painting. One of the companies who made the kits had reached out to her and offered a small monthly stipend to create content. With the end of the month approaching, she owed them another video.

"Maybe we could do a movie tomorrow, then," I suggested as compromise. Even when she wasn't trying, my fiancé was perfect.

"Works for me," both parents said, nearly in unison. Excellent.

"Tomorrow it is," I exclaimed. I retreated upstairs, changed into my hiking clothes, and slipped out the back door as the sun was gathering its rays, making ready to nestle down under the western horizon. With one last glance over my shoulder, I made sure no one was watching from the windows, then slithered down to the rocks to retrieve my tools... weapons, I corrected myself.

"Call a spade a spade," I muttered to myself. "Or, rather, call an axe an axe."

With my defenses in tow, I practiced moving as silently as possible, every footfall deliberate. Deliberate movement was precise, and true precision was deathly silent. Supplanting myself against a lone rock, I took in the street stretched out beyond the forest.

The sunset cast wild shadows across the woods, and only spackled light danced over my position. Ray of 126 Slate was not yet home, I inferred from his empty driveway. The atomic twins were home from work, though; Fatman's pearly-white pickup sat in the driveway at 124 Slate and Little Boy's ragged Jeep rested in front of 123, the house across the street. The jerk had parked it with two tires kicked up on the lawn.

Despite the tangerine glare of sunset, I could see the enormous flatscreen TV glowing through Butch's front window. I saw the familiar sidelines and yard markers of a football field. So, I sat... and waited... and tried to watch some of the game through Butch's window.

The sun went down as I crouched there in the soil, dousing the woods in harsh shadow. A crisp breeze cut through the trees, bringing with it the fresh scent of colder weather. At one point, I saw Butch stick his fat nose outside and scan the front street. He may have looked inconspicuous, but his robotic body language reeked of guilt and lascivious intentions.

To a bystander, Butch was just peeking outside to check the weather – like the groundhog Punxsutawney Phil. They had a lot in common: the portly bellies, the hairy shoulders... nah. I waved the metaphor away. It was unfair to groundhogs.

Butch squinted as he peered up and down the drive, then finally retreated inside again, careful not to let the screen door slam. Interesting – he'd let that door slam at least twice as they were leaving that morning. He was being extra discrete.

I wished I had a GoPro or two, as I could have mounted them along the tree line to monitor the situation remotely – possibly record any misdeeds these two fools got themselves into. But with my luck, I'd miss the real damning evidence due to bad camera placement or a corrupt video file. Not to mention that I didn't have the resources for that fancy setup.

Finally, about forty-two minutes after dark, Ray returned home to 126 Slate Drive. His headlights prodded at my hiding spot as he guided his Toyota into the driveway. I went unseen as he shut the car off and sat in it for a moment, no doubt gathering his belongings. As he swung the driver's door wide, the car's headlight warning drifted to me on the wind, dinging at Ray until he switched them off.

Over at 124, I saw Jim's pointy nose poking through

Butch's window blinds on the side of the house.

Ray traipsed slowly up his sidewalk, in no hurry at all. I knew that walk: the workday was still heavy on his shoulders.

Jim was gone, the blinds rocking so slightly, it could have been a breeze. The air was cold, especially for August in North Carolina. The wind moving through the trees felt like November chills in the Midwest – unbridled by any breaks in the landscape, and liable to cut right through clothes and stiffen the joints.

Ray produced his keys and fussed with the lock at his front door.

No changes over at 124.

He muttered to himself, then the door swung wide, flooding his yard with lamp light from the foyer.

Still no changes next door.

Ray ducked inside and closed the door. The action was punctuated by the cartoonish thunk of his deadbolt.

Then, I simply waited. How long, I cannot say, but it was a while. Long enough, in fact, that I was starting to think perhaps Butch and Jim had lost their motivation. Thank God for that...

As if on cue, Jim was at the front door at 124 again. He scanned the street, noted Ray's Toyota, then ducked out of the entryway again.

Just a couple minutes later, he returned to the front door, Butch in tow behind him. As they stepped outside, I saw that Jim was carrying a plastic cupcake container– one of those clear pastry holders from a grocery store bakery.

What the hell, I thought. What, exactly, was their plan?

If poisoned food was involved, these two were even dumber than I thought. It would, however, be much easier to intervene. I pulled out my phone and opened the camera. Jim held the container high, like he was presenting a sacrificial lamb, and as the streetlight caught it, I could see that it was, indeed, cupcakes.

They rang the doorbell – Butch did. Strange, I thought. He was wearing gardening gloves. So was Jim. I touched my own gloves, realizing why I had chosen to wear them. Fuck: these two were serious, I had no more doubt. But how? I needed to know their plan if I was going to thwart it.

Ray came to the door.

"Evenin', Ray," Butch yukked like a schoolyard bully trying to make nice. "Where's Ella?"

Cautiously, Ray cracked the door ever so slightly.

"With her mom for the weekend," Ray said. "Y'know how it is." From my position, I could still see a chain lock in place. I also glimpsed the line Ray was treading socially. Polite without seeming suspicious.

"What, uh…" he didn't finish his words, but gestured to Jim and the cupcakes. He did not open the door further.

"Oh," Jim said, his voice singing like a cherub's, "we just brought ye' somethin' sweet."

"A peace offering," Butch said, pointing back at Jim's decaying Jeep.

"Oh," Ray leaned back, his brow raising almost to his hairline. "That's very kind – I appreciate that very much. Here – uh – well, I hate to ask, but…"

"What is it, neighbor," Butch cooed, his tone and body language invoking memories of Earl Sinclair, sitcom TV's favorite overweight Megalosaurus.

"Does that have any nuts in it? Can you check?"

"Uh," Jim started. "I don't frankly know how to check. Could ya' step out here and show me?" There was the plan. They were trying to lure him outside or be invited in, I wasn't sure which. I saw Jim glance over at the woods.

Ray's door was slowly closing.

I readied my phone camera. "May the forest protect me," I prayed to no particular god. I think I was merely appealing to all goodness in the wild world.

"If there's any trace of nuts, I could be headed to the

hospital just by getting near those. I'm sorry. I don't mean to be rude, but I can't risk it."

I pulled the hosiery over my face and pulled the hood of my black sweatshirt up over my head.

"I got it," Butch chimed in, taking the cupcakes. He seemed shaken from nervous paralysis as he witnessed the scene before him, much like an actor unwilling to commit to their part. Demonstratively he held up the plastic case of sweets and read the label. "Warning: risk of cross-contamination with peanuts and tree nuts."

"Yeah, I can't even be around that. If it has traces of peanut, my face will balloon like the Stay Puft Marshmallow Man." to his credit, Ray tried laughing at his own expense to lighten the mood. Butch and Jim reacted like two goons who'd never seen Ghostbusters; they just stared at Ray. "I'm, uh… I'm just gonna'–" Ray didn't finish. He just shut his front door.

I watched the sides of Jim's mouth curl from a sickening grin to an agitated scowl. "Nut allergy," he whispered. "Fuck me sideways."

"Sorry, Ray," Butch called out. He lowered the cupcakes, staring down at them thoughtfully.

"Shit, we coulda' left 'em on the front porch," Jim guffawed. "Put 'em in an unmarked box next time – problem solved!"

"Shut up," Butch said wearily.

"You know what," I heard Jim offer. "It's not a total loss. If you give me the receipt, I can take those back for store credit–"

Butch did not miss a beat. He turned on a dime – as fluid as a high school athlete – plucked one cupcake from the tray of half a dozen, then smashed the remaining five cupcakes into Jim's face in one swift blow.

"I said *shut up*," Butch added. Then, with textbook precision, he ended his child-like tantrum by stuffing that preserved sixth cupcake between his trembling jowls. He marched back up his own lawn and through the screen door with a violent, rattling slam.

Jim staggered back, inhaling frosting as he prepared to shriek. Before he could exhale his string of expletives, however, I shifted, and bumped into the pickaxe. The sickening, empty clunk as the wooden handle fell over betrayed my presence.

Jim twitched, gurgled like a rabid demon pup, and his waist turned on a swivel like a man possessed. He drew a pistol from his belt and aimed it into the woods...

... in my direction.

I threw myself to the ground, huddling behind a tree. Shaking with nerves and adrenaline, I pulled off my facial hosiery, grabbed my weapons, and vaulted over a fallen tree for better cover.

"Who's in the woods," Jim growled. "I saw ya' in there." He smeared frosting from his forehead with the back of his arm as he tried to wipe it out of his eyebrows.

Then, he leapt into the woods after me. A flash of light in his wild pupils told me right away that he had spotted me, though his gun was currently caked in frosting and smashed back into his holster.

13. DEATH'S PURPOSE

Adrenaline rocketed through my system – it felt like Surge rocketing through my innards at a childhood pizza party. Most likely, that was due to the shakes it produced… that and the churning in my gut.

I pushed straight back into the forest twenty paces or so, then cut northwest, my knees wobbly as bricks of jelly. I was headed in the direction of Grāf's campsite.

Should I involve my new friend in the toils of man? Would I jeopardize Grāf's safety if Jim went missing and there was an investigation? Wouldn't the woods be crawling with cops? I couldn't help but snort. My new favorite spot, spoiled by clumsy pigs. How apt.

It was too late to change my mind, for the campsite was upon me in an instant… and it was abandoned. I recognized everything, even in the dark. The way the rocks were stacked against a half-fallen tree – the way the stream trickled past. Yes, it was the right spot; I could see the low green glow of Grāf's portal in the tree trunk.

Something was off – no Grāf, no pile of firewood. The fire ring was still there, though.

When I was practically on top of the gelatinous membrane, I shuddered. The passage's surface area had reduced in size and luminance. It had been glowing fiercely upon my visit the night before, but now it flickered like a dying Christmas bulb.

Why had Grāf so hastily returned after our meeting?

Was it something I said?

I suppressed my disappointment.

"Damn spiders," Jim cussed as he trampled through a web only fifteen paces away. He stopped to swipe them out of his face, squirming while he went. I uttered a silent prayer of thanks to the busy arachnids around us.

Ten more paces, then he shuddered to a halt and slapped his hands on his knees, huffing and puffing within six feet of my position. He must've overdone it chasing after me. That meant he wasn't as healthy as he appeared.

Good.

I did not move. Did not breathe.

While he was sucking air, I melted back into the shadows. What happened next, I still cannot fathom. Jim reached in his back pocket and produced a smartphone. I saw the screen cast harsh shadows across his angular features, even heard the ringing on the line.

"What," a reduced voice snapped over the tiny speakers. The labored mouth-breathing was unmistakable to me. It was Butch.

"Hey man," Jim hissed in an ineffective whisper. "Stop being a baby and get out here."

I couldn't make out Butch's reply.

"I think it's that kid I told you about. I don't want 'im to get away – he's out here spying on people an' shit."

Butch's words were still unclear, but the tone was obvious. Fat Man wasn't coming out to play. Little Boy rolled his eyes. "Fine." He hung up. "Lard ass," he muttered as he put the phone away.

He pulled his gun from its holster and flicked away another lump of frosting. As he cleaned more of the clumped sugar from the muzzle, I saw that it was some sort of antique 19th Century revolver – Civil War era – with a modern silencer affixed to the end.

Goddamn this cretin, I thought.

Next, Jim plucked six bullets from a pouch on his belt and fed them into the chamber. It hadn't been loaded earlier... interesting.

"C'mere, lib-tard," he crooned to himself, not realizing I was practically upon him. "I'm lynchin' something tonight!"

With that, Jim sealed his fate. I heard in the sickening soprano notes of his leering all the worst of humankind.

Deceit.

Hatred.

Stubbornness, privilege, insolence...

Self-righteousness.

Abuse.

Such poisons attacked me through Jim's siren song. I could hear every paper-thin argument ever proposed to keep the south's precious Confederate 'heritage' in-tact. I remembered how effortlessly this bumpkin spat the N-word, tossing it around like a twelve-year-old kicking a tattered hacky sack.

He was disease to me. The middle-aged man hounding me in the forest was a failed organ transplant. He needed to be rejected properly for my species to survive.

When a tooth goes bad, do we not still pull it?

When a finger is moribund, do we not still amputate?

Why then, should the whole of human progress suffer at the hands of slovenly, racist idolators? Must we continue to bestow such pig-headedness with privilege due solely to a lottery of chance wherein the greatest prize is a shriveled, dispassionate member?

We the species are the whole of the plant; should we not trim back the putrid leaves that threaten the rest of our branches?

Thunder rumbled out west, but it was Death's hissing voice that broke my trance.

"The stage is set," he warned. With his words, I understood that it was time for Jim to meet his miserable end. In that moment, Death lifted the veil shrouding perspective and obscured my field of vision with memories. They were projected like eight-millimeter films across my contact lenses, complete with emotional recall, as though I was their owner, but I recognized none of them.

A different boy – different childhood – different stories – played out all at once for me. The boy was auburn haired with features worthy of *Children of the Corn*: too many freckles and an upturned mole nose. I staggered, understanding in an instant how severely rotten James V. Abernathy was. He was spoiled corn, turned potent long ago, and it was written in every strange, unspeakable memory forced upon me. A lust for underdeveloped young girls, disturbing pleasure while hunting and skinning animals, and Klan meetings since the fifth grade were only a few of the highlights. To share even half his miserable woes would take a lifetime. Were I to revisit them in detail, it may very well rupture my mind.

Suffice it to say, I saw him plain as day; he was perfectly twisted in every worn out, First-World way. A shyster whose only goal was profit – who saw other people as objects to be used for cash or gossip or pleasure. Then there was the most damning sin of all these, and Death plunked it into my brain with punctual precision. Jim thought he was better than other people… thought he deserved more.

The sensation left my sinuses tingling, crammed suddenly full of pins and needles. I sniffled, wiping away the snot, trying not to think of Gräf's disgusting sneeze from the night before.

Jim grumbled to himself, pulling my focus.

A raucous bolt of adrenaline rushed through my system.

Jim was a cavity, and Mother Earth wanted a root canal.

It was dark – I checked over my shoulder – the nearest house lights were all but lost, nothing more than glimmering fairy tails hovering over the pond.

Just by the darkness of that cloudy, moonless night, I knew I had him. My night vision was acute, despite my terrible short-sightedness, something that countless roommates had commented on over the past ten years. I could see distinct outlines of all that familiar terrain. I knew the woods, and they knew me.

Another shot of adrenaline.

The forest gathered in, propelling me to act – it demanded the sacrifice.

First, eliminate the gun.

I grabbed two fist-sized rocks from Grāf's fire ring, one in each hand. I threw them deep into the woods out north, far from my position. One cracked off a tree, the other clattered off a much larger rock.

With a yip of shock, Jim twirled. He emptied his chamber into the shadows.

I rolled my eyes.

Six shots in all – and they seemed muffled compared to the loud *crack* each bullet made when it buried itself in the hide of my oaken shields. I heard the familiar *click, click, click* of an empty revolver chamber. Jim was, for the moment, out of ammo.

Because he was staring off to the north, he never saw me coming. In thirty seconds, I was on him, cutting in from the right, swinging the hatchet low, at Jim's shooting hand.

I barely aimed, just watched the butt of his gun as I closed in. The blade struck the gun with a slink-chunk, the gun dropped, and a spray of crimson spattered the ground. Jim tackled me, squealing like a possessed mongoose. In my shock, the hatchet tumbled away. I tried to fling it far from us as it fell.

Jim pulled my face close as he toppled me. "Skateboard fag," he exhaled sadistically.

We landed, our heads knocking against each other, and bolts of white light jumped at me from the night sky. Then, everything went dark.

ଔ   ଌ

Thunder shook me from my dizzy trance. Though the night sky was gloomy with clouds, stars danced over my head as I fought a mild concussion. I reached out for balance, noting that I'd smacked my head off a rotting tree stump...

Jim groaned next to me. Reflexively, I scanned the dark for any glint of metal and there, between our knees, was his damnable pistol. I snatched it up and hurled it off into the trees. The exertion of whipping my hand around so quickly summoned a barrage of head pain.

By sheer luck, I managed to dodge Jim's clubbed left fist. I struck his knee from the outside with a right punch of my own. We stumbled back to our feet, each waiting for the other to make a move, each glaring daggers across our verdant arena.

"What," he challenged.

I didn't scare him, but that was fine by me. Because there, in the shadows behind him, I saw the familiar shroud of Death watching over us. Then, my heels knocked against the pickaxe, and I finally accepted it; I was merely Death's instrument.

It was time for a solo.

Hefting the pickaxe, I planted my feet.

Finally, the foreboding clouds ripped open overhead with sweet relief, baptizing my tool. Thunder let loose, and lightning eased my squinting for a moment. But it blinded Jim, and I took a swing. He flinched, his arm knocking the axe around in my hand before the blunt edge glanced off his jaw with a crack.

Jim dropped to the wet forest floor with a yelp, but not before his defensive flails knocked the tool from my hands. Miraculously, the pick hit the mud with a wet smack less than three inches from my foot.

My victim groaned in the mud. He forced himself over onto his hands and knees, the dead leaves clinging to him like he clung to a heritage of hate. I toed him in the ass, and he flopped over. His hands were empty – he wasn't hiding another weapon.

Good.

I whirled around and pulled the pickaxe from the mud, but it was enough time for Jim to lurch back onto his feet.

Bad move, Jim.

I swung the sharp end of the pick at Jim's head. I missed as he leaned back, flinching in surprise. Instead, the pick grabbed the soft skin above his clavicle. With a wet, metallic slink, I spiked him clean through the base of the neck.

Then, I felt the pickaxe grind against his bones, the sound reverberating up through the wooden handle… and right to the knot in my throat. I dry-heaved, but Jim didn't see it.

His eyes had rolled back into his head and his mouth fell slack. He didn't even have a chance to plead for mercy. His arms flailed, his knees gave out, and he collapsed backwards.

Death glanced up at the sky, and a crash of thunder muffled the screams.

The weight of Jim's struggles on the pickaxe tried tugging me forward, but instinctively, I tugged back. With a crack that made me dizzy in my gut, Jim's head jerked up hard, bobbing off his right shoulder. It swung from a thick tether of torn muscle and t-shirt as the pickaxe ripped it halfway off his body.

The blood began to pour, but so too did the rain. It washed Jim's venom from me like suds down a drain. I slipped on wet leaves, turned to face Jim again, but his body collapsed in front of me. He gaped in horror like some cognizant lab experiment who finally realized he was a monster.

But I was only Death's tool... only human.

"I'm sorry," Jim tried to whimper. In a crack of lightning, I saw the tears in his eyes. I couldn't stop now; I was past the point of no return.

Somewhere deep down, I felt the cracks of my psyche spiderweb like breaking glass. I shut my brain off, and for whatever reason, my long-lost thespianism took over.

"To die, to sleep," I droned to myself. "To sleep? Perchance to dream," I went into a trance as I swung the pickaxe down at Jim's heart. "Ay, there's the rub; For in that sleep of death what dreams may come..." another swing of the axe. "...when we have shuffled off this mortal coil." Jim shuddered one final, ragged gasp, and died in front of me. The last thing he heard was the Bard's greatest lament; one little taste of culture before his candle was snuffed out.

I turned away, trying not to vomit as I rejected the images of ragged red flesh. Tears of horror rolled freely down my face, lost in the falling rain. I was panting for breath – didn't think I'd been wounded. Though, as the adrenaline wore off, I could feel a dull hammering on my temples. It made the blood in my ears run hot as radiator steam.

A biting breeze rattled the trees, whisking Death up next to me. That misty shroud exhaled, almost a sigh. "Do you see now?"

I did indeed see; Death was human nature.

He dissolved into the gathering fog, and that was the end of our dealings...

                                     ಐ   ಐ

We are an instinctive species, and in the moment of action, I had not considered the possibility that I might have to dispose of a body. I suppressed my wild panic as it screeched inside me like some demented parakeet.

I just needed to breathe.

I wished I had my pipe.

I wished Grāf hadn't left. They were nowhere to be found, and something in my gut just knew they'd gone back through the portal.

My thoughts shuddered to a halt.

The portal was still there. A portal to another world on what I could only assume was another planet. That was it! I'd cram the cadaver through that snotty membrane! But I would need to test that theory. Even though I assumed Grāf had passed through already, I didn't know for certain whether I could push something from my world through. There was only one way to find out.

I steadied my resolve. It was time to clean up.

Swallowing my distaste for the scene, I chopped Jim's head free, knowing it would be easiest to carry, and therefore to experiment with. If I simply put the body through Grāf's portal, along with my, er... weapons – then the likelihood of anyone ever finding me out was drastically reduced. I didn't know much, but I knew that propelling carrion into another realm somewhat complicated legal hearings.

I had not counted on the portal being so small. It was only large enough to feed a cadaver through on its side, if at all. It would still work, but it would require that I balance Jim lengthwise on one of his arms. I kept the cursing in my head so as not to tempt the spirits of the night.

I grimaced as my fingers stuck to Jim's forehead. The dead skin was clammy in the humidity. I shoved his skull into the portal with disgust, letting go before my fingers touched the gooey membrane.

"Alas, poor dipshit. I knew him well." It didn't make me laugh. The barrier wavered, the surface color of the portal shifting to a rich sour apple green where the head made contact. As Jim's wild white mane passed through, the membrane belched a scent of burning hair. I stopped breathing through my nose.

Did the edges of the passage contract a bit?

I swore they did.

Next, I found the hatchet in a tangle of underbrush and pushed that through the strange membrane. Again, the surface shivered sour green and the edges of the passage closed in as it accepted the hatchet.

The portal's membrane was definitely decreasing in size as it accepted physical objects. That's why it was smaller, I realized. Grāf went back through sometime today, perhaps even as soon as we parted ways. It was only then that I realized I would never see them again, for it would be far too small after I shoved the corpse through. My heart was heavy, but I shook the feeling.

No time to focus on that; I had a body to move.

I wanted this to be over: needed it to be. I grabbed Jim by the shoulders, able to grasp his overalls like handles. There was just enough of a neck stump left to keep his overalls in place, thank God, and the excess moisture clung to him. He slipped and slid with me most of the way.

Getting him into position was rough, but eventually I worked it out. I started by trying to feed him in headfirst, but the missing head made leverage hard to accomplish. I'd line the shoulders up, but as soon as I'd step toward his feet, his stump would slide free of the membrane. Finally, I swung his corpse around and shoved him in feet-first. This went much easier until the portal closed in around his waist, trapping just his bump of a belly and his mangled bust on my side of the passage. Without hesitation, I stuck a heavy foot in his gut, compressing it forcefully. Some unpleasant flatulence echoed through the cadaver from the other end of the portal, and I suspected I'd applied too much pressure, so I stopped.

Oof. Sorry, Grāf, I thought.

I shifted my position, then shoved again, and Jim slipped through to another world, leaving the ripped fabric of space-time no wider than a laptop screen.

I saw by the re-emerging moonlight that my hoodie had been stained a devilish crimson. No more risks, I thought as I grabbed my gardening gloves and the pickaxe. Next, I wrapped them in the hoodie, stripped down to my underwear, and wrapped everything up. The whole bundle was pushed through at the same time. I stood a moment, checking the scene. The physical evidence of my disturbing deed was suddenly immaterial.

I took my time getting home, letting the rain cleanse my skin. My phone, of course, was fried from all the water. It was a small penalty, and I did not complain. I was careful with my key, moving it into the keyhole tooth by jagged tooth. I put pressure on the back door to prevent the hinge from squeaking and slipped upstairs into the shower undetected.

挈 択

When people go missing, communities notice. The inquiries kicked up throughout the neighborhood about four days after that treacherous night. They lasted only a week...

Apparently, one of Butch's neighbors got irritated with Jim's Jeep and had it towed away at dawn, so Butch didn't realize his friend was missing until he was already a suspect.

Since both Butch and Jim had been working on our street, the police came by our block and questioned nearby neighbors. With the family gathered round, I explained to them quite plainly:

"I recognize the man in the photo as a construction worker from the job two doors down. While I never interacted with him firsthand, I did notice him coming and going from work with a heavy guy in a big white Ford pickup."

The detective shot a glance to the officer accompanying her. Standing in the corner, the officer crinkled his chin with conviction.

"I think he lives somewhere around here, too," I added.

"I saw him riding around on an ATV one night with a shotgun strapped to his back…" I caught myself, remembering the phone call Jim had made to Butch. He had mentioned me… sort of. He mentioned a kid.

"…while I was out with the dog," I concluded for extra cover. "Scared the shit out of me, frankly, which is why it stands out," I shared. The officers laughed.

"He was trouble," the officer said knowingly.

Oh?

"Thanks for your time," they concluded.

And so, life went on.

We weren't downstream of the gossip mill, so it took some time before we heard more. Authorities suspected Jim had run into foul play as a result of his own shady dealings. The unlicensed guns in his impounded Jeep further fed that flame. The woods were allegedly searched, but nothing was ever found of him, save the remnants of a small campfire. Either he had run away or got lost somewhere. His wife Maggie hated his guts and his kids had disowned him, so there was no one to mourn his loss. A sad end to a sorry excuse for a human. The spiders of the forest had spun me an alibi for the ages.

Despite it all, I struggled with nightmares until I adapted. Eventually, the visions of flesh tearing – reminders of the person I'd torn apart – conformed to hexing me only in the early morning hours. And I already preferred to be up in time to watch the sun rise. It allowed me to focus on the day ahead… to take stock of what was lingering in the shadows before they were swept away with the sun's incoming tide.

My fiancé and I were married about a year later and we chose to settle north. The first morning in our hillside apartment, I awoke before daybreak to discover a massive marbled-orb weaver, or Araneus marmoreus, quilting a web across our office window. In North Carolina, I had stumbled upon a few of these, but they were never bigger than the bulbous tip of my pinky finger. This specimen had an abdomen the size of a dime. Surely it was a good omen; my friends, the arachnids, were keeping watch for me, still.

I smiled, and my instinct was to leave it be – I even watched it work for a while as I sipped my coffee. Then, reminding myself that our window was on ground level right next to the complex's main entryway, I grew concerned that someone might clobber the beautiful beast. I set about gently scooping it into a mixing bowl, marched it dutifully into the woods, and set it free.

In fact, I've made a habit of doing so with every spider I find in the house, vowing never to treat them like intruders.

After all, the woods were here first. And, though the forest seemed foreboding and perilous, man would ever be its deadliest intruder... the ape who spends his life spreading Death.

Surely, Mother Earth would reject us soon.

EPILOGUE

If we shadows have offended
Think but this and all is mended,
That you have but slumbered here
While these visions did appear.
And this weak and idle theme,
No more yielding but a dream,
Gentles, do not reprehend:
If you pardon, we will mend:
And, as I am an honest Puck,
If we have unearned luck
Now to 'scape the serpent's tongue,
We will make amends ere long;
Else the Puck a liar call:
So good night unto you all.
Give me your hands, if we be friends,
And Robin shall restore amends.

-Puck, Act V, Scene 1; *A Midsummer Night's Dream*
Shake-Speare

ABOUT THE AUTHOR

{photo credit: Dale McCarthy @dmdarkroom}

Award-winning author Gerald de Vere was born and raised in the haunted hills of Pittsburgh, Pennsylvania in a time when technology was a decade behind the trends. In that sense, he has lived a somewhat old-fashioned life, relishing in the study of history, biology, psychology, and art. He holds bachelor's degrees in English and in Theatre, as well as a master's degree in Creative Writing, all achieved at Black Swamp University in Ohio. When he's not scribbling, Gerald enjoys restoring vintage collectibles and roaming the North American wilderness.